A MESSAGE FROM CHICKEN HOUSE

Are you ready for the Olympics? OK, how about next sports day? When you've got a chance of winning, what comes first? Friendship or places on the podium? This thrilling sporting mystery takes you to the heart of this question, and is bursting with authentic action (author Eloise is a former Olympian!). With cheating, bullying and sabotage, who *really* wins in the end?

BARRY CUNNINGHAM
Publisher
Chicken House

Eloise Smith

WINNER Takes

GOLD

Chicken House

2 Palmer Street, Frome, Somerset BA11 1DS
www.chickenhousebooks.com

First published in Great Britain in 2024
Chicken House
2 Palmer Street
Frome, Somerset BA11 1DS
United Kingdom
www.chickenhousebooks.com

Chicken House/Scholastic Ireland, 89E Lagan Road, Dublin Industrial Estate,
Glasnevin, Dublin D11 HP5F, Republic of Ireland

Cover and interior design by Steve Wells
Typeset by Dorchester Typesetting Group Ltd
Printed in Great Britain by Clays, Elcograf S.p.A

1 3 5 7 9 10 8 6 4 2

British Library Cataloguing in Publication data available.

PB ISBN 978-1-915026-30-9
eISBN 978-1-915026-31-6

To children who dream
and adults who cartwheel.

1

THE SPARKLY GRAVESTONE

'How you doing today, Mum? I've something to show you. Watching?'

Pearl raised her arms to the cloud-streaked June sky. A breeze fluttered through her dark, shiny ponytail. Feet together, she focused on a line of trees at the far end of the cemetery. She blew out through dimpled cheeks. This was the hardest part of her tumble sequence. The part she kept getting wrong. And which most twelve-year-olds would never attempt, even on a tumbling floor.

She began her sprint. Despite her small frame, she quickly built speed. She moved powerfully along the grassy avenue dividing the rows of graves. She counted five perfectly measured steps before launching into a front handspring. Her fingers pushed off the newly cut grass, still damp with morning dew. Blood rushed to her head, but she was used to it. Her body locked as she flipped in the air. Landing, she flew back up. For a moment, she was weightless. Just limbs, joy and energy. Glittering granite and sky flashed past. Mid-air, she curled up. Her knees crushed against her chest as she spun. *Release now*, whispered the breeze. She straightened out as the ground hurtled towards her. Just in time, her feet connected with grass, in front of the last gravestone.

Her body compacted down. She half-stepped forward, steadying her position. She frowned, hoping the error wasn't obvious. Then flexed her arms up in a 'V', waiting for applause. A front handspring tuck deserved a clap, even with a tiny mistake. Mum's gravestone remained silent. Pearl sighed and let her arms drop.

Fishing in her tracksuit pocket, she pulled out a tube of superglue and a single silver sequin. She unscrewed the cap, taking in the inscription on the stone:

Renshu Chui-Bolton
Wife to one,
Mother to two,
Inspiration to gymnasts,
Ray of sunshine to all.

She carefully glued the sequin over the 'i' in 'sunshine'. It joined a throng of sequins adorning the inscription. One for every visit. Twice a week for a year now. She popped the cap back on the superglue and surveyed her handiwork.

'Getting much cheerier.'

Mum didn't disagree. Pearl looked around the cemetery. The other graves looked tired: wilting flowers, weather-bleached photos, a discarded bottle. Not like Mum's – Bagley End's brightest gravestone. It had fresh carnations too, that were magically changed every week. Pearl wasn't sure who by. Certainly not Dad, who was too busy with his extra shifts to visit very often.

She slipped down into crossed legs. She put her shoes back on, taking her time. She cleared her throat.

'So, Mum. Thing is . . .'

She paused, straightening her feet in front of her.

'What if I don't get selected for the squad?' The words tumbled out, fast and awkward.

A bee buzzed in the grass.

'I mean. I should. I will. I have to!' she gabbled. 'I've done enough training, haven't I?' Though no training was ever enough to know for sure. Not even twenty-five hours a week. The gravestone didn't respond. However, Pearl knew exactly what Mum would be thinking.

'Light up the world with your shine,' Mum had said on the last video call, before the doctor's masked face appeared, serious eyes masking nothing.

'I'll shine brightly for you, Mum,' said Pearl quickly, nodding at the gravestone. 'I'll win gold in Paris, just like we dreamt. I won't let you down, I promise. Whatever it takes.'

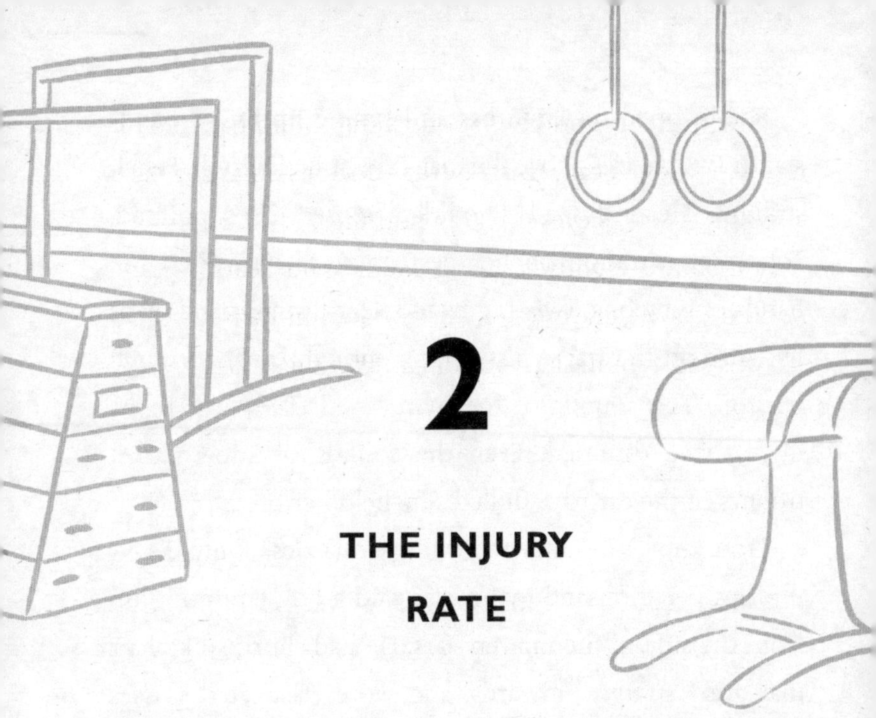

2

THE INJURY RATE

Bagley End Butterflies wasn't the best-equipped gymnastics club ever, nor the biggest, and it certainly wasn't the most successful. No one there had ever made it to the GB Mini Elite Squad, let alone the International Cup. Once, though, it had been Mum's home-from-home. As a coach, she'd spent countless hours within those four breeze-block walls, helping Pearl with her tumbles, landings and corrections. She had touched every part of it, from the faded crash mats to the practice-smooth pommel horses to the ancient water cooler. It all held a tiny part of Mum. Which was why, for Pearl, it was the best club in the world.

She gripped the high bar and swung up into a handstand. Two metres above the mats, she stilled herself. Pencil straight. Head dipped. Shoulders tensed. Toes pointed. Total concentration on her best event. She reversed her hands one by one, twisting round. Her leather hand grips felt sure on the bar – just grippy enough, not too much friction. The sounds of the gym faded. The strip lights high above dimmed. Even the sounds of supermarket trolleys in the car park dulled. She held her breath.

'You know the injury rate in gymnastics? Only 0.687 injuries per thousand gymnasts,' said a boy, squinting up from the side of the uneven bars. He had short, spiky hair that grew straight upwards, and wore elasticated glasses strapped to his eyes. 'Much safer than horse riding and rugby.' This was Ryan Stone, Pearl's best friend for as long as she could remember.

'That's not helpful right now,' said Pearl, trying to regain focus. She locked her eyes on the lower bar.

'I find it relaxing to know,' Ryan mumbled from below. 'Might mention it in my next podcast.' His podcast, *Flipping Without Falling*, was on its twenty-fifth episode and had precisely two followers, one of whom he was related to. He wiped his chalky hands on his baggy shorts then held them up to spot her. He stood, knees soft, stomach forward, ready to support.

Pearl concentrated, then let gravity swing her into a forward giant. Her grips slid smoothly round the bar. Wind whistled past her ears. She whooshed back up to vertical. A holding pause. As she spun again she released. Airborne, she spread her legs into a straddle, rolling backwards while flying forward.

She crunched into the lower bar, catching poorly. Her legs whipped up. Panic surged. Ryan was under her in an instant, grasping her flailing legs. He clutched her hips clumsily to help her dismount. Pearl toppled down on to the mat, white-faced. That was close. Too close.

'Still think the backwards straddle roll should be in my routine,' said Pearl, pulling her leotard back into place. 'It'll help my difficulty scores. And I'm mainly getting it.' Mum would have pushed her to keep it in.

'But you need to be one hundred per cent getting it,' said Ryan, adjusting the stretchy strap on his glasses. 'Just keep it simple. Make the top eight, you'll qualify. That's how I'm seeing it.'

'No one made the Mini Elites keeping it simple,' snapped Pearl, immediately regretting it.

'Maybe,' sighed Ryan, not taking offence. 'But you know how my mum worries.' He looked over to where his mum, Gloria, was helping the beginners do forward rolls. Pearl felt even more guilty. Once the club organizer, Gloria had stepped in last year as coach. She tried her best, but she wasn't half the coach Mum had been. She'd got worse since her nightmares about Ryan falling had started.

Ryan made his way towards the parallel bars. His feet pointed inwards as he walked, almost as if he was shy of his own gymnastic capabilities.

'Sorry,' called Pearl, following him.

'It's true, though,' he replied. Chalk dust billowed up as he straightened the mats. He eyed the bars gravely.

'Talking of upping difficulty scores, I should try my double tuck dismount again.'

Pearl raised her arms, ready to spot him. Ryan retucked his singlet into his shorts, tight against his stomach. He took a step forward and a jump up. He swung into his routine, placing his hands with clockwork timing. Ryan was never the first to try a difficult move. However, those he mastered were textbook perfect. He moved like he had in-built ball bearings. Every turn was performed with mathematical precision; every angle was exact. He spun up into a handstand, straight as a ruler. His mouth twisted to the side, chewing the inside of his cheek.

'You can do it!' Pearl called in her sunniest voice. 'Go on, push yourself!'

A second ticked past, then he swung down, his toes cutting a perfect semicircle in the air. He released into a tuck. A single tuck. He landed squarely, legs compacting before straightening. His definition was strong. His dismount was clean. But it was definitely not a double tuck. The bell sounded. End of their last session. His shoulders relaxed.

'I'll do it when I'm ready,' he said with a shrug. Then sprinted across the gym. 'Last one to pack up gets the back seat,' he called. Pearl laughed and jogged after him. She dodged out of the way of the taekwondo students streaming in.

Tomorrow, it was the trials. And they were going to totally smash it. They had to. There was no other option. As a shimmer of doubt chased after her, she sped up.

3

THE BOX OF TROPHIES

For Pearl, like her mother before her, gymnastics was everything. So it was no surprise that her bedroom was a shrine to somersaults and saltos. It contained proof of every success she'd ever had: on bars, beam, vault and floor. She'd run out of shelf space for her trophies, so her latest ones were neatly stacked in cardboard boxes under her bed. They sat beside another box of medals that were too painful to display. The walls were covered in grade certificates, rosettes and shiny medals. Not forgetting, of course, the posters of her many gymnastic heroes. They smiled down like sporting saints, blessing the room with their bendy brilliance.

The June sun was only just setting, but the curtains were already drawn. Pearl needed to be well rested for tomorrow. Max sat cross-legged on the duvet, in his dinosaur onesie. Pearl had already done teeth-brushing with him, combed his ever-messy hair, read him three picture books and sung him his favourite of Mum's lullabies. He angled the bedside light up at the wall.

'So, who's that, again?' he asked, pointing at the biggest poster. He furrowed his brow with surprising concentration for a six-year-old. Like he was studying for an exam in Big Sister Bedroom Wall Trivia. Sitting in a splits that took up all the available floor space, Pearl looked up. She knew she didn't need to be stretching just before bed, but it made her feel more relaxed. She took in the poster. It captured a flying gymnast, body flexed like a swallow, crowds out of focus behind. Her blonde locks were cropped short. Her pale blue eyes glimmered with gold eyeshadow. Her old-fashioned white leotard was striped with blue, yellow and red. The colours of Romania.

'Elena Cazacu. Only the greatest gymnast of the last generation. More Olympic medals than you can count. She invented the Cazacu, a super-famous beam dismount. It's a backwards layout with double twist.' Max nodded earnestly, as if he knew exactly what this was. 'She's the best coach around now, Mum trained under her at Leaping Spires.'

She flopped down beside Max on the bed.

'I'll probably get to meet her if . . .' She didn't need to finish the sentence. Max knew. If she made the Mini Elite Squad.

A knock at the door. They stopped talking. Dad peered round, dressed in a navy company uniform, a pile of laundry under his arm. He looked tired, like he'd grown another wrinkle.

Max gave Pearl an earnest, wet kiss.

'Good luck tomorrow,' he whispered, so Dad couldn't quite hear. He scampered out quickly, well aware it was past his bedtime. Dad sat down on the edge of the bed. He didn't ask about practice. He never did any more.

Pearl slipped under her duvet.

'Sorry I can't take you to the trials,' said Dad, after a long silence. 'It's tricky with my extra shifts.'

Pearl nodded. Gloria would take her, like she always did, now Mum no longer could.

Dad stood up, taking in the sagging shelves.

'Maybe we should have a clear-out soon?'

'Soon,' said Pearl, crossing her fingers under her duvet. No way were her medals going anywhere. Not hers. Or Mum's. Dad put a hand on a shoebox full of trophies.

'Could free up some space for other things?'

'No!' Pearl had meant to say it, but it came out as a

shout. Dad took his hand away.

'Might be good for you to do something other than training once in a while. See friends? Go to the movies? Hey, we could even go to the seaside, if you like? We could get a beach hut. You could cartwheel on the beach like old times?'

Pearl shook her head. Dad didn't understand. She had a friend, Ryan, and she saw him all the time. She watched movies. She'd seen *Summer of Somersaults* and *Summer of Somersaults* 2 a gazillion times. And the seaside? Like she had time for that when she had medals to win.

As Dad closed the door, he sighed. He sighed a lot these days. Especially when it came to gymnastics. Which was difficult, because it was all Pearl thought about.

4

THE PLATE OF BEANS

At six a.m. the next morning, the sun was still in its pyjamas. Pearl, however, was not. Under her track-suit, she was already wearing her lucky competition leotard. It was light blue with a 'P' hand-sewn on the chest in plastic pearls by Mum. It was also slightly too small, but no matter. Her dark, shiny hair was in her neatest ever bun. She even had eye make-up on. Across the cul-de-sac at Gloria's, she was having her pre-competition breakfast. Because in just a few hours the trials were starting.

'Eat up,' said Gloria. 'We need to be out of the door in ten, or I'll be in a right flap when we arrive.' She filled the dishwasher quickly, controlling her jumpiness with high-speed tidying.

Gloria's kitchen was a small but highly productive space. Organized down to the last Tupperware box, it held a surprising number of useful gadgets and well-labelled leftovers. With Dad's long shifts, Pearl had all her breakfasts and weekend lunches there. She loved Gloria's purposeful bustling and her industrial-scale fruit-cake making. What she loved most of all, though, was the feeling of being fussed over. It reminded her of how home used to be.

Pearl pushed the baked beans around on her plate, pretending not to be nervous. Ryan looked over from his breakfast. Under his glasses, he looked puffy-eyed, like he hadn't slept. Even his spiky hair was a little less sharp than normal. Neither said anything. They didn't really need to talk anyway. Pearl knew how Ryan would be feeling; Ryan knew how Pearl would be feeling. That was the thing about them. They'd known each other since they were babies. As toddlers, they'd mastered their forward rolls together. Then on to cartwheels and the splits, always with Mum cheering them on and Gloria wringing her hands.

He finished his beans and stood up. The chair legs scraped on the vinyl floor. He stacked his plate and gave the countertop a wipe down.

'I'll do that, Ryan. Go and brush your teeth and do your

affirmations,' said Gloria, taking the cloth off him. 'All of them.' He groaned and left the kitchen, banging up the stairs in protest.

'He's not like you,' said Gloria, starting on the cheese sandwiches. 'The nerves really get to him,' she added, looking like the nerves had already got to her.

Pearl chewed slowly on an edge of toast. Her stomach was a hard knot.

Gloria paused her sandwich making. Her short curls bounced to a halt.

'Pearl, real athletes eat. And that' – she pointed a finger at the plate – 'is sport fuel.'

'Can't. Too excited.'

'Excited or worried?' said Gloria, pointing a roll of clingfilm at Pearl.

'Not worried. I have a really good feeling about it. I had a dream last night I'd already qualified for the Mini Elite Squad, then won the International Cup in Paris. I was sitting on the podium eating gold ice cream. And the King and Queen were clapping from their VIP box.' Pearl didn't mention who else had been there in her dream – a woman cheering proudly, with shiny, black hair and a dimpled smile just like hers. 'Probably a sign from the universe that I just absolutely can't fail, right?'

Gloria raised an eyebrow, unconvinced.

'Today, if you don't make the top eight, it's not a failure, OK? Even qualifying for the trials is a success. Especially since it's your first time out of Compulsories. I don't want you to be disappointed. Just be careful how much pressure you put on yourself.'

Pearl gave Gloria a big, sunny smile to put her off the scent.

'The sun doesn't always shine, Pearl. No point pretending it never rains. Sometimes you've got to put your hand out and feel the rain on your skin.' Pearl nodded politely. Honestly, though, she had *no* idea what Gloria was talking about. None. It wasn't raining. There wasn't a cloud in the sky. And she knew for a fact there wasn't a shower due all day, which was pretty unusual for Wales.

Upstairs, the rumble of an electric toothbrush was replaced with the mumble of Ryan's affirmations.

Shaking her head, Gloria called up the stairs:

'Louder, Ryan – you can't half-believe your affirmations.'

Ryan's volume increased.

'I, Ryan, am full of potential. I, Ryan, trust my grip.'

Pearl looked at the shelf on the far wall. At the end of a row of plastic storage solutions was a framed photo of Mum and Gloria in light-blue tracksuits. The best friends looked young and happy, with matching belly bumps, at the door of Bagley End Butterflies, on opening day. Pearl looked down, blocking out a surge of sadness with a large forkful of beans. What if she fluffed up her routines? What if she let Mum down? The thought was too painful, so she pushed it away, along with her plate.

The affirmations got louder as Ryan swung down the stairs.

'I, Ryan, believe in Myself. I, Ryan, am a Winner.'

He landed firmly, but his eyes dipped with worry as he caught his mum's glance.

Gloria grabbed her minibus keys and hurried them both out of the door. Pearl took a deep breath. The trials were happening, and it was time to perform.

5

THE GOLDEN MIST

Chatter, applause and the hopes of two hundred children bounced around the sports hall. On the tiered seating, parents clapped and took photos. In the central area, gymnasts twirled and tumbled, pulling off acrobatic moves with steely smiles. Cardiff Sports Centre had never seen so many sequins.

Pearl sat on a bench, jigging her legs nervously.

'Pearl Bolton on Range and Conditioning,' the PA system blared. Her first rotation of five. Pearl stood up. She smoothed an imaginary wrinkle from her leotard. This was it.

Gloria put an arm around her shoulder as they walked

over to the floor area.

'However you do, it's a success, OK?' she said. Pearl took in the long table of unsmiling judges. They didn't look like they would agree.

'Wait!' Ryan jogged, pigeon-toed, after them.

'You've got this,' he said, holding out his fist.

Pearl grinned. They bumped fists, releasing in an exploding hand motion. Trust Ryan to remember. The same superstitious routine they did every competition. It always brought luck. As Ryan jogged away to warm up for his own rotations in the other sports hall, Pearl felt a flush of confidence.

She began the first routine of her first ever squad trials. As she lifted and held, twisted and leapt, the luck seemed to flow through her body. From straddle press to handstand and into a bridge, the moves connected fluidly. She felt strong and sure, like gravity was her plaything. All else was forgotten, except the elastic joy of gymnastics. She finished with a flourish. The judges nodded, impressed. She beamed with relief as her scores appeared.

The rest of the events unfolded like a daydream. Pearl pummelled her floor routine, nailing every tumble. Her vaulting was foot perfect. On bars, she soared, performing powerfully on her best event. She pirouetted, released and transitioned like a flying fish. Only when she dismounted did she notice she'd drawn a crowd. As Pearl stepped off the mats, lungs bursting, a girl stepped forward. She had big eyes, neat braids and a tiny frame. Pearl recognized her instantly from *Gymnastics Monthly*. Jada-Rae Williams. At just thirteen years old she was already tipped as an Olympic hopeful.

'Hey, what's your secret?' Her smile was wide and goofy. 'I should take notes!' She opened a tiny, white notebook, joking like she was about to write Pearl's response in it.

'Huh?' Pearl undid her hand grips, confused.

'No one from the squad's ever seen you before, and suddenly *that*.' She pointed up at the far wall. 'Pretty cool. A medal contender!'

Pearl looked up. On the far wall, attached high up for all to see, was a digital scoreboard. On it eight names were illuminated – the girls currently in position to make the Mini Elite Squad. And there, blinking hopefully in fifth position, was a name that made her heart sing.

P. Bolton – Bagley End Butterflies

Now only the final rotation stood between her and selection for the Mini Elites. It would be goodbye to club gymnastics, hello to a whole new world of top performance. A month-long training camp at Leaping Spires. There'd be state-of-the-art facilities. The newest equipment. The best coaches. And at the end, the chance of making the team for the International Cup in Paris. Her dream glittered in a golden mist across the arena, waiting to be realized.

6

THE DOUBLE TUCK DISMOUNT

'Can't believe how well you're both doing,' said Gloria, passing round an open Tupperware. Her eyes were bright with nervous excitement. 'I'm so proud of you both.' She gave Ryan a one-armed squeeze, before hurrying off to double-check the scores.

Ryan, back over during a break in his rotations, shrugged and bit into his sandwich. Pearl could see he was pleased, though. Nothing made him happier than when his mum forgot her many worries about his sporting abilities. Even if it was just for a minute.

Sitting in splits on the floor, Pearl nibbled on a sandwich. She put it down.

'Don't tell your mum, but I'm going to finish with my double tuck.'

'Why would you do that? And on your weakest event?' Ryan wiped mayonnaise from the edges of his mouth, shocked. 'You've never done that in competition. My mum said you weren't ready. And she's your coach now.'

'But I could medal from here,' said Pearl, eyeing the scoreboard. 'Why wouldn't I push myself?'

'You're in position to make the squad. Keep it simple. Just stick to your routine.' He fiddled nervously with the stretchy strap on his glasses.

Pearl frowned.

'Why would you risk messing up such a good score? Statistically speaking, gymnasts are more likely to fall on their final event.' He widened his eyes like a puppy. Pearl gave in. How could she refuse her best friend, who just wanted her to succeed safely?

However, as her name was called, and as she dusted her hands with chalk, the possibility of medalling called to her. She could do more than scrape into the Elites. She could win gold. What a way to join the squad that would be.

Arms stretched. Fingers splayed. Feet together. She steadied herself in front of the beam. A metre and a quarter high, ten centimetres wide and five metres long, it stood waiting for her. She swallowed, mouth dry. Behind, music played as another young hopeful began their floor routine. Far in front, a powerful gymnast took a run-up to the vault. She glanced to the side. On the bench sat Gloria and Ryan, hands clasped in sporting prayer. Behind them both, on the front row of the stadium seats, perched a sparrow-like woman. The head coach of not just the Mini Elites, but the Junior and Senior Elites too. Elena Cazacu.

She was older than the poster on Pearl's wall, but otherwise unchanged. Her blonde hair was still cropped short. Her eye make-up was still heavy and metallic. And she still shimmered with excellence. She watched Pearl, pen hovering above a golden notebook, eyes beady with focus. Pearl's stomach flipped.

She began. Her mount was clean and graceful. Up on the narrow beam, she moved smoothly into a tiptoe walk, dipping, kicking and hand-flicking all the while. An arabesque followed a backwards walkover before she swept into her leap series, lifting and dipping like a wave. A crouching pirouette. Then to the acrobatics section. She spun and flipped like a shower of rainbows. Standing at the end of the beam, her pulse raced. Only the dismount to go, the crescendo of a so-far-perfect routine.

Until she decided to do the double tuck dismount, after all. Forget keeping it simple. This could be a medal-winning dismount. It had seemed impossible a few hours ago. But now? Could she medal? After all, she was wearing her 'lucky' leotard. And today, she was feeling a high-difficulty score kind of lucky.

A bend forward. A push through the knees. Toes pushed off suede. She was airborne. Pushing up high, like a swallow. No, a swift. Actually, a hummingbird, because they can fly backwards. The strip lights high above seemed to strobe as she flipped. Her fingers gripped her thighs as she tucked in tight. Ceiling became floor; floor became ceiling. Heels over head; head over heels. Faces in the crowd rushed past. And among them, a face that she couldn't have possibly seen. A woman with dimples just like hers. An impossible wish. Concentrate! A slight twisting. Then straightening out to land. Ahem . . . then straightening out to land.

Pearl felt a whooshing. The bad kind. She struggled upright. Too late. A half-scream. *Thwack*. Pearl hit the mat, spine first, head cracking back. Pain rippled through her body. Then a silent, shooting blackness.

7

THE BLINKING SCOREBOARD

'Don't move, please. My name's Dr Pond, Chief Medic.'

A steady voice emerged from the blackness. Lying on her back, Pearl opened her eyes, shockwaves from the fall still radiating through her. She gazed past the concerned faces of Gloria and Ryan, over on the tiered seating. Miss Cazacu was gone and so was her golden notebook.

A broad-shouldered, rosy-cheeked medic squatted down beside her. Wearing a pristine tracksuit and expensive-looking, immaculate trainers, she looked like she had been freshly unwrapped from sterile packaging. She checked Pearl's neck in a well-rehearsed motion.

'Does this hurt? Any numbness? Tingling?'

'No,' said a small voice in Pearl's throat.

'What about here?' Dr Pond worked her way down Pearl's torso with precise, freshly scrubbed hands. She lifted an arm gently.

'Here?'

Pearl gently shook her head. She didn't dare look around, but she knew every gymnast in the competition would be watching to see how bad the injury was. Was it ice-pack-bad or hospital-bad? Would gymnastics be over for the surprise newcomer?

'OK, it's not spinal. But you were out cold, you'll need to be checked for head injuries. How many fingers am I holding up?' Dr Pond held up two fingers. Or was that three?

'I think I'm fine, honestly,' said Pearl, struggling up. A pain shot up her left ankle. It was like glass shards and boiling water. She cried out, her leg buckling under her.

'Whoa, you're not going anywhere,' said Dr Pond, catching her. Pearl caught a whiff of perfumed soap as she lay down again.

Kneeling in front of her, she pressed the inner side of Pearl's ankle. Pearl winced. Her ankle throbbed. But worse was the front-row view she had of the beam. Where any number of gymnasts could now easily beat her score.

'Push against my hand,' said Dr Pond. Pearl pushed the ball of her foot down.

As the next gymnast completed her beam routine, a lump formed in Pearl's throat. *Don't cry.* Up on the blinking scoreboard, another name replaced hers. The tide of pain was replaced with a flood of regret. A perfect chance, lost. Her dreams of making the Mini Elites disappeared in a puff of stupidity. Despite nine years of gymnastics. Despite training twenty-five hours a week. Every week. Even school holidays. Despite missing every birthday party ever so she could train. Despite everything. Her eyes welled with tears. She stiffened as she felt a sob shudder through her.

Dr Pond paused. She looked at Pearl through earnest, grey eyes.

'I was a rower in my youth, not a gymnast. One thing I know, though. There's more to gymnastics than scores.'

Pearl bit her lip. Being up there on the scoreboard would have made Mum so proud. It would have made everything OK for once. But she couldn't tell an adult she was totally wrong. Could she?

'What about friendship? Building character? Or just the feeling it gives?' suggested Dr Pond. 'Your routine was special, you should be proud of it.'

'Thank you, Dr Pond,' Pearl said, 'but I'd swap all that to have made the squad.' She turned her face away, embarrassed by the tears drifting down her cheeks.

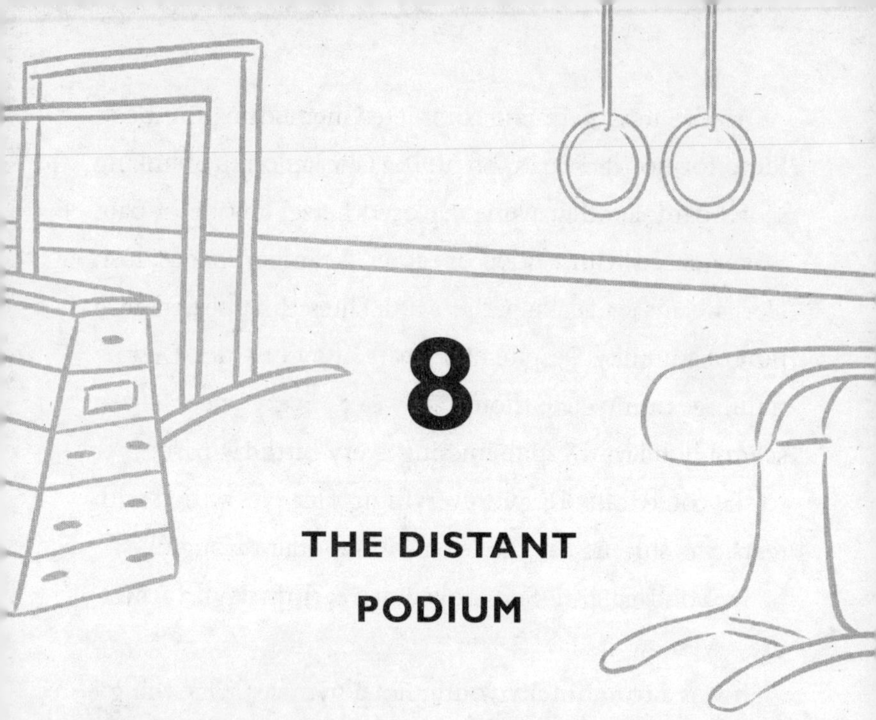

8

THE DISTANT PODIUM

Pearl sat alone in the bleacher seats, staring down into the sports hall. It was being prepared for the medal ceremony. Miss Cazacu was directing the placing of the podium. A block for bronze, a slightly higher block for silver and the highest block for gold. All the places Pearl was not going to be taking. She had dreamt of medals and making the squad, but instead she had a sprained ankle and bruises. She held an ice pack to the back of her head, nursing an egg-shaped lump. Her ankle was strapped up, with strict instructions from Dr Pond to follow R.I.C.E. for two weeks. As in Rest, Ice, Compression and Elevation. But definitely no training.

Ryan sidestepped along the seating to her. He had changed into jeans, swapped his elasticated glasses for his off-duty ones and his spiky hair was towel-dry. He held a Tupperware of Gloria's finest fruit cake and two bottles of orange Fruitogade. He sat down in silence, handing her a bottle and a slice.

Pearl crammed fruit cake into her mouth, washing it down with Fruitogade. The raisiny sweetness and tangy fizz distracted her for a moment. She dropped crumbs on her light-blue Bagley End Butterflies tracksuit and left them to linger. She couldn't bear to say anything to Ryan. And he knew it. It was too annoying that he had been selected, not her. Too irritating that he'd just kept it simple and made it through.

'Really well done,' she said eventually, trying her best. 'Imagine – you're one of the Mini Elites now. In the squad! Camp will be amazing. A whole month at Leaping Spires. The chance to try out for the International Cup team! Think of the content you'll have for your podcast. Wow.' She flashed Ryan a big smile. She was trying really, really hard to show how happy she was for him, but Ryan caught the sadness in her eyes.

He unwound the zinc oxide tape on his fingers, now damp from his shower. It protected from rubs and rips, so Ryan used it religiously.

'Won't be the same without you,' he said, studying his hands. 'Who else will listen to my gymnastics stats?'

Pearl stared down at her crutches, smarting.

'In bronze place, Aashni Patel and Ella Hart,' introduced the announcer.

A small, powerful-looking girl made an explosive leap up on to the block. Her thick mane of black hair was tamed into zigzagging plaits. This was Aashni Patel – a.k.a. Lightning Girl, thirteen years old and already an unbeatable tumbler. There was something fearless about the way she tilted her chin up, eyes drawn back in her head like a wild horse's.

'There's always next year,' said Ryan, picking the tape glue off his fingers.

'I'll be too tall. Can't be a gymnast with a high centre of gravity,' said Pearl, eyes trained on the pixie-like, even-featured gymnast approaching the podium. Ella Hart. Aged thirteen, she already had thousands of followers on social media. She skipped on to the block, hugging everyone she passed. With her blonde, coiled plaits and iridescent, heart-patterned outfit she looked like a spangly fairy. She received her flowers and medals, giggling and taking selfies all the while.

'Statistically speaking, the tallest ever female Olympic gymnast was one metre seventy. Anyway, you might not grow.' Ryan wasn't used to being the one doing the cheering up, and he wasn't very good at it.

'Erm . . . have you met my dad?' snapped Pearl.

'True. But your mum was the perfect gymnast's height.' Pearl looked at Ryan. He'd broken their unspoken rule. Mum should not be mentioned any more.

'I think I just want to be alone, if that's OK,' she said, voice wobbling.

Ryan got up, looking relieved. He walked away, more pigeon-toed than ever. Pearl turned back to the ceremony, feeling like the loneliest girl in the world.

'In silver place, Isla McMorrow,' continued the announcer. A precise, red-haired girl stepped up. Face neutral, she dipped her head for the medal. A red-haired boy in the crowd cheered; she nodded coldly.

'And in gold, for the second year running, Jada-Rae Williams.'

On to the podium jogged Jada-Rae, all wide eyes and an even wider smile. Pearl watched as if through unbreakable glass. She wanted all of it. Their shiny tracksuits. Their confidence. Their impossible skills. She would have given anything to be one of them. Just like Mum had once been.

9

THE EXPLODING FIST BUMP

Pearl stood in goal in the front garden with Max. It was drizzling but he'd insisted. She tried to bat off another penalty with her crutch but failed. Scoring, Max cheered. Pearl sighed. His love of football was so simple. He wasn't even in a team, but he didn't seem to care. He was always winning the FA Cup in his head, and that was somehow enough for him.

Across the cul-de-sac, Ryan trundled a giant suitcase round to the back of Gloria's minivan. This was the day Pearl should have been leaving for camp. Instead, he was.

'Aren't you gonna say goodbye?' said Max, retrieving the ball. Pearl shrugged. She and Ryan had hardly spoken for two weeks. He had been busy training; she'd been busy being fed up about not training.

They watched Gloria wheel a second giant suitcase round. Ryan was never one to under-prepare.

'She still angry you changed your routine?' asked Max, doing keepie-uppies.

Pearl shrugged again. She looked down at her ankle, tested it with a little bounce. Gloria slammed the boot door and made her way round to the driver's side. Ryan hovered, checking the rainy sky.

Pearl sighed into her crutches and began the long walk across. The swelling had gone down and her ankle felt better. However, she was taking no chances on the last day of her two weeks of enforced rest. The rain fell faster. It splattered down, turning her tracksuit a darker shade of gloomy. She manoeuvred around a parked car, eyes glued to the wet tarmac.

Pearl and Ryan stood looking awkwardly at each other, not quite knowing how to say goodbye. They never hugged and now wasn't the right time to start. Max ran up, face flushed. He barrelled into Ryan, giving him a goodbye hug.

'We'll miss you loads. Especially Pearl,' he said.

Pearl looked embarrassed.

'You've got this,' she said, holding up her fist. They

fist-bumped, releasing hands in an exploding motion.

'Bye, then.'

'Bye.'

Max scampered back across the cul-de-sac. Ryan got into the minivan thoughtfully. Gloria started the engine. Pearl hurried to the driver's side. Gloria unwound her window.

'I'm sorry, Gloria. I shouldn't have changed my routine like that.'

'You know, everyone makes mistakes. The best gymnasts have made more than you've had hot dinners, but it's what they learn from those mistakes that matters. So that next time, they get up and do it better. Now, enough beating yourself up, OK.'

Pearl hung her head as they drove away. There might not be a next time for her. Not if she kept growing. Tumbling was much harder with long legs. She made her way back to their house. Normally she would count the walk in cartwheels, but not today. There didn't seem any point.

She made her way down the hallway, swinging on her crutches. Snaking around stacked boxes and an overflowing laundry basket came the smell of dumplings. Dad was in the messy kitchen at the back, standing over a spitting pan in his navy uniform.

'I'm doing your favourite.'

Pearl forced a smile. However, her failure at the trials weighed stone-like on her shoulders, refusing to budge. It felt like her world had caved in, and she was just watching it collapse on her. She leant on the fridge and stared at the ceiling. Her dream was officially over. How could she shine now? Gymnastics was how she shone.

Dad's mobile buzzed on the counter. He handed her the spatula and took the call.

'Hello? Yes, I'm Pearl's father. Who's speaking?' he said, walking out into the hall.

Pearl poked the crisping dumplings. Three minutes from frozen to parcels of perfection. Crispy on the outside, squishy inside. The best comfort food in the world. They weren't like Mum's home-made dumplings, but still. She looked up as Dad came back in. He looked weary.

'That was the head coach,' he said. 'Elara Caza something?'

'Elena Cazacu!' Pearl clasped her hand to her mouth.

'That's right. She was very complimentary about your performance. Before your fall, that is.'

He wasn't going to say what Pearl thought he was, was he? She put down the spatula so she could cross both fingers.

'She was offering you a place at camp.'

Pearl squealed. Her shattered dreams unshattered, re-forming in a twinkling glow in her mind. This was big. A second chance! She ran over and jumped up, hugging him like a baby koala. Dad brushed her down.

'There's a *but*, though, Pearl.'

10

THE TOSSED CRUTCHES

The kitchen seemed to quieten, the pan of dumplings straining to hear what Dad would say next. He looked at Pearl sadly.

'I can't let you go.'

He sat down, pulling a chair out for her. Pearl remained standing, her heart in freefall. The words crashed against her ears. She couldn't move.

'I'm sorry. It's not a good time right now. It's a lot of money that we don't have, even if it is subsidized. Where would I get an extra grand and a half from? I'm already working too many shifts.'

'Gloria will know what to do. I'll ask her,' pleaded Pearl.

She sniffed. Something was burning. Her eyes flicked to the spitting pan, where dinner was fast being cremated. The dumplings would have to wait.

Dad shook his head.

'It's more than that. I need your help here. Max needs his big sister,' he said, trying to take her hand. 'Plus, you're only just recovering from injury.'

Pearl threw her crutches on the floor.

'I'm totally recovered.' She squared her shoulders and stood tall. She raised her arms towards the ceiling. She fixed her eyes on Dad and furled her fingers out. This had to be the best pirouette she'd ever done. Extending a leg, she kicked off. She spun on her recovered foot, toes pressed into the floor. Dad watched her, transfixed. Pearl rotated her straightened leg around in a steady horizontal spin. She circled past sink, fridge, hallway, burning pan, then returned to Dad.

The dumplings were smoking now, but Pearl wasn't stopping. She spun round again and again.

'Stop!' Dad's voice was firm. 'Pearl, I don't want you to go. I don't want you to injure yourself any more. What if you hurt yourself worse next time? I can't bear to lose anyone else. We've lost enough already.' Dad's face was broken with tragedy. He sighed, long and slow. 'I'm sorry. I wish things were different.'

Pearl's dream shattered all over again.

'Mum would've let me,' she shouted. Though she knew it was wrong, she ran to her room and slammed the door.

11

THE BIG SUITCASE

The street lights had just come on, making pools of light in the cul-de-sac. Pearl stood at Gloria's front door in her pyjamas. Behind her the minivan's engine still ticked as it cooled, freshly returned from dropping Ryan off at camp. Otherwise, it was quiet. She rang the doorbell. Gloria would help, she had to.

It was a few moments before the door opened. Gloria was in her nightie, hair in a towel, holding a cup of something warm and malted. Pearl barrelled into her.

She gabbled an explanation, but before she was finished, Gloria had put her coat on. Still in her slippers, she grabbed her house keys and marched out of the door.

Pearl rushed after her in the direction of home. Hope tugged at her heart.

Pearl's house was dark except for the flicker of the TV in the front room. Upstairs was quiet, Max sleeping soundly. Gloria rapped on the window.

The door opened. Dad was in his dressing gown. His eyes were red. He looked confused to see Pearl.

'How did you get outside? I thought you were asleep?'

Noticing Gloria, he blushed. Gloria eyeballed him, hands on hips. She had a determined look in her eye. It was showdown time.

'We need to talk, John.'

Before Dad could welcome her in, she was past him, past the overflowing laundry basket and into the front room. Dad followed her back in, shutting doors in her wake. Pearl pressed her ear to the door.

'I know it's difficult for you, but your daughter has talent. Have you seen her handsprings? Her tucks? It's like the girl is made of rubber bands and electricity. She has to go.'

'It's a grand and a half I don't have.' The volume on the television was turned up.

'That can't be a reason.'

'Things are hard enough already, Gloria. You know that.'

'What about if I said we'd get the club to chip in? We've built up a little cash buffer for emergencies. And what is this, if not an emergency?'

The room was quiet but for the TV.

'And I can help with Max and pick-ups.' Gloria was not a woman who took 'no' for an answer.

'What if she gets injured again? Renshu said when she trained there half her squad broke bones.'

'I worry too, John, all the time. I don't want Ryan to get hurt, but that's gymnastics.'

Pearl strained to hear.

'You know, every mention of gymnastics reminds me of Renshu. I can't bear it.'

'I miss her too. She was my best friend, my business partner. But she would have given everything to see her little girl succeed.'

Dad sighed, as if he had the lungs of a whale.

'I'm sorry, I can't.'

Footsteps moved towards the door. Pearl crept up the stairs and curled up in bed to nurse an entirely broken heart.

That night, Pearl had a dream. She was running across a plain of dried-out mud under a blistering sun. Sprinting, but oh-so-slowly. Her body had a strange heaviness. Bright flashes and jangling surrounded her. Hanging from every part of her body were gold medals – from her neck, her arms, her wrists, her knees. They tripped her, twisting on their ribbons; they blinded her, flaring in the sun. Hearing a cry, she looked up. Outlined against the sky stood a woman. She was small and slight, with shiny, black hair and dimpled cheeks. She stood alone.

Pearl ran, weeping. As fast as she could sprint, great openings appeared in the mud between her and the woman. She leapt over them, medals clattering, lashing her in the face. More cracks kept growing, spreading out in huge zigzags, slicing up the landscape. Pearl pulled up in front of one the size of a canyon. She screamed after the woman. All she knew was that she must not stop. Not now. Not ever. She jumped forward, across the chasm she could never cross.

She was falling.

Tumbling down.

Knocking rocks.

Still falling, she woke up.

There was a thudding coming from above. She checked the clock. Two-thirty a.m. A dull scraping sound echoed above. Pearl pushed the duvet back and crept out of bed into the hallway. The attic ladder was down.

'Hello?'

Dad's head appeared through the hole. He held a large suitcase.

'Guessed you'll be needing the big one. A month is a long time.'

Pearl howled with happiness. She raced up the creaking rungs to hug him. Again and again, because she knew how much she'd miss him at camp.

12

THE GLITTERING GLASS

It was early afternoon by the time they drove through tall, spiked gates and up a long, wooded drive. The conifers on either side were densely planted, giving away no secrets. Pearl's stomach fluttered with excitement and service-station food as they parked on the forecourt.

She hopped out of the minivan as Gloria turned off the engine. The air had a cold, shivery tang to it. However, it was July, officially summer, so she was wearing shorts. She rubbed the goosebumps on her legs briskly.

As Gloria unlocked the boot, Pearl took in her new home. Mum had told her stories about the illustrious Leaping Spires – the National Gymnastics Centre. It looked even more impressive than she'd imagined. Surrounded by a neatly cut lawn with a lake to the side stood a vast, glass structure. It was like a greenhouse on a growth spurt. Giant mirrored glass panels were edged with freshly painted white metal frames. A peaked glass roof magnified the weak northern sun, making the building sparkle. This was the place where gymnasts were turned into stars. Mind whirring with possibilities, Pearl turned to help Gloria wrestle the suitcase over the gravel.

'At last!'

At the top of the steps stood a woman with impossibly long eyelashes, and an even more impossibly long pony-tail. Wearing full make-up and a candyfloss pink, silk tracksuit, she looked like an artist's impression of a sporty fairy godmother.

'Welcome to Leaping Spires!' She paused to glory at the shimmering building. 'Built on the site of a Victorian hospital, inspired by the hothouses of Kew Gardens, funded by our generous sponsors, Fruitogade.' She pointed at a vending machine by the double doors, full of yellow, orange and pink energy drinks. 'Now populated by the country's best young gymnasts, this is where Mini Elites become Junior Elites, and Senior Elites become Olympians.'

She bounced springily down the steps, bubbling with energy.

'I'm Lulu Sweet, call me Mrs Lulu. Artistic Director of Leotards, Choreography Consultant and qualified Smile Coach. Oh, and Miss Cazacu's assistant, of course. Miss Cazacu will teach you all the moves, but I'll bring the dazzle to your performance!' Pearl smiled, feeling a little bedazzled herself.

'Now I don't mean to hurry you, poppet, but Miss Cazacu's camp briefing is in the floor gym in thirteen minutes. And she has extremely high standards, especially around punctuality!' She winked winningly.

'Your settling-in buddy can take you from here,' she said, putting a shiny-nailed hand on Pearl's shoulder. As if on cue, a red-headed girl dipped through the double doors. Pearl recognized her from the trials. Isla McMorrow. The Star of Scotland. In a tracksuit zipped up to the throat, and with not a hair out of place, she wore a blank expression.

'Oh, I don't mind helping her settle in,' Gloria said breezily. 'Pop in on my boy?'

'Gymnasts and staff only inside. Miss Cazacu is very private about her training methods.' Lulu shrugged apologetically. 'I am sorry. I know how it feels, I was once a gym parent too. My daughter used to train here. Anyway, I'll give you a minute to say your goodbyes.' She took a few discreet steps away.

Gloria enveloped Pearl in a perfumy hug, squeezing her tight.

'Don't forget to enjoy yourself, OK? We're all very proud of you. Me, your dad, Max . . .' Gloria was not a woman who ever paused. For a moment though, she did. 'Your mum would have been too.' She patted Pearl's shoulder and cleared her throat. 'Tell Ryan to keep doing his affirmations and believe in himself!

'Oh, nearly forgot!' Gloria nipped back to the minivan and retrieved two large Tupperware boxes from the passenger seat. 'Extra fruit cake for you both.'

Behind, Lulu coughed.

'Sorry to be a fun sponge, but anything sugary is banned.' She rolled her eyes sympathetically. 'Not my rules!'

Gloria looked deeply shocked, but took the Tupperware boxes back to the minivan. Pearl stood waving as Gloria did a twelve-point turn.

'Thank you,' she whispered after her. Gloria double-honked back as Pearl skipped up the stairs to join Isla. This was going to be the best camp of her life and she couldn't wait to get started.

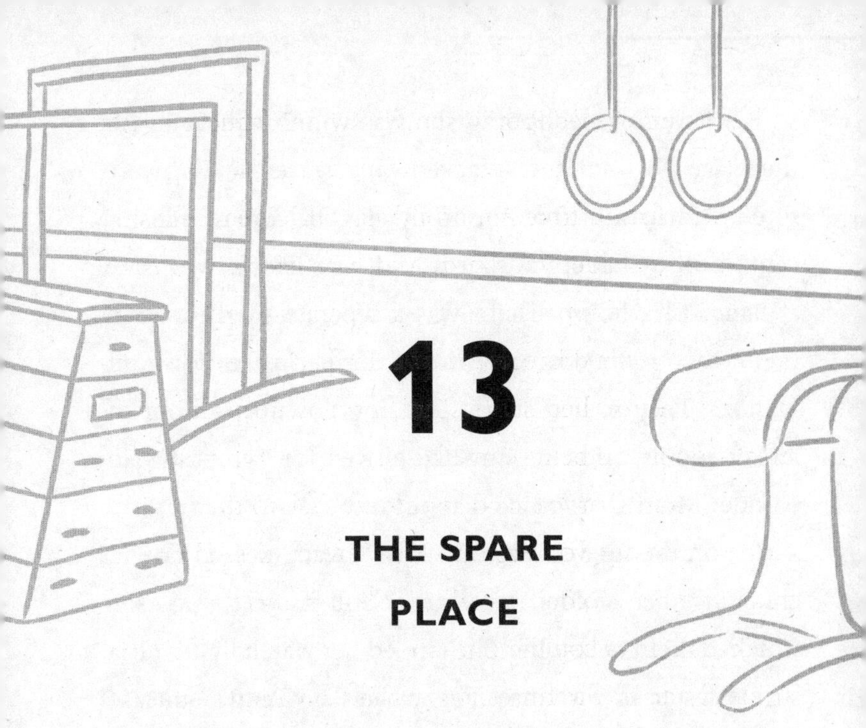

13

THE SPARE PLACE

Inside the building was a spotless, four-storey high atrium. The air was moist and scented with citrus. Isla walked fast, not looking back. Pearl followed in single file, dragging her suitcase. They passed raised beds planted with fruit trees.

'Are those orange trees? And lemon? Look!' said Pearl, trying to start a conversation with the back of Isla's head. Isla was taking being tight-lipped to a whole new level. Pearl looked up to read silk banners hanging down from the top of the glass ceiling:

FRUITOGADE
The Winning Taste

Pearl swallowed, hoping she was winning enough for the place. To each side, stacked on terraced levels, were three gymnasiums, broken up by glass balconies, translucent flooring and spiral staircases. It was like being inside a giant doll's house. There was a separate gym for each event, each with gymnasts already limbering up for their sessions. They passed stairs spiralling down to a floor of locker rooms below. It was like heaven for gymnasts. No wonder Mum always talked about it.

Up on the highest balcony, Miss Cazacu peered down, clutching her golden notebook. Still as a statue, she watched them below her. She tapped her watch lightly; Isla strode faster in response. The wheels on Pearl's suitcase clattered over the freshly mopped tiles as she sped up too.

'Wow! She's so serious!' Pearl whispered in awe. This time, Isla responded. She spoke without slowing her pace, spitting out the words like apple pips:

'Her pupils have won gold, silver and bronze in the International Cup every year for the last twelve years.' Isla charged through the far doors into a gleaming hallway. It was a hall of fame, lined with trophy cabinets and framed photos of gymnasts from throughout the years. From grainy black and white, to the faded browns of seventies photography, to megapixel modern photography, every winner was captured.

'When she worked for the Romanians, they won.'

Throngs of gymnasts from eleven to eighteen streamed the other way, moving with precision. Pearl had never been around so many like-minded, leotard-loving kids.

'When she worked for the French, they won.'

The trophies gleamed in agreement.

'Now she works with us, and she expects whoever gets picked for the Cup team to win.'

They passed a brightly lit canteen to the left and a door marked *Rest and Recovery* to the right.

'So, yes, she's serious,' snapped Isla, coming to a curved stairwell. A large sign read: *No handstands. No cartwheels. No backflips.*

'Wahoo!'

Two flights up, a shiny-haired lad slid down the banisters head first. His arms were held out behind like a skydiver. It was Mo Varma. The superstar of the Mini Elite boys' squad, with boy-band looks and unstoppable confidence. He shot round a bend. Cat-like, he landed on the tiled floor, winked and sprinted off down the hall of fame. Wow. Pearl watched after him, momentarily distracted.

'But maybe it's not so serious for you,' tutted Isla. 'Since you're only here because Zoe got injured before she'd even unpacked her bags.'

Pearl froze. What?

'Oh, did you not realize? Miss Cazacu had to fill the spare place. You're just the last-minute replacement.' She sniffed, smoothed back her already smooth bun, and mounted the stairs, two at a time.

All the way along the girls' floor, the fresh cut of Isla's comment stung. As they hurried to the furthest room, it bruised and bled. Did she really deserve to be there?

'You're taking Zoe's bunk,' said Isla, holding open the door.

'What happened to Zoe?' said Pearl, dumping her suitcase on the lower bunk.

'Curse of Leaping Spires,' replied Isla, hanging off the door. 'You never know if you'll end up on the podium or in hospital here.'

'Huh? That's a joke, right?'

Isla smiled, as coldly as a shark, and shot off again. Pearl grabbed her gym bag and rushed after her, brushing away the painful feeling that she didn't deserve to be in the squad.

14

THE GOOEY LEOTARDS

The Mini Elites' locker rooms were huge and sparklingly clean, fragranced with air freshener, bleach and hairspray. Gymnasts chatted, adjusted leotards and clipped back stray locks. On the wall a digital timer bleeped loudly. A ticking countdown began. 05:00. Five minutes until the briefing. The girls streamed upstairs towards the gymnasiums above. Pearl dashed along the lockers, searching the name plates. Twelve names. But no Pearl.

'That's yours now,' said Isla, pointing at a locker at the end. The name plate read: *Zoe*. Of course. As if she didn't already feel like a last-minute addition. She shoved her gym bag in and wriggled as quickly as she could into her training leotard.

'Hurry up, you'll make me look bad,' sighed Isla. 'Just like my twin does.' She slammed her own locker door and departed with the exiting gymnasts.

Pearl straightened up. She blew out her cheeks.

'Ignore her. She's proper snarky with everyone. Lucky you're not Hamish. He gets it the worst.' A small but powerful-looking girl stood in front of her, dark ponytail swishing, lightning-patterned leotard shimmering. Pearl recognized her. Aashni Patel, Lightning Girl. 'You need to be hard as nails for this squad, but you don't need to be a mega-moo. Right?' She seemed friendly, in a tough kind of way. She chewed her gum slowly, taking Pearl in. 'I remember you from the trials. Thought you crashed out?'

'I did,' said Pearl, the memory a gut-punch.

'Huh.' Aashni blew a slow, pink bubble. It popped.

The pitch of the timer increased. 03:00. Three minutes to go.

'Let's go. Miss Cazacu loves any excuse to tell me off. If I wasn't such an awesome tumbler, she'd kick me off the squad.' Aashni did a running leap up on to the benches, cartwheeled along them and tuck-jumped fearlessly off the other side. Pearl grinned at her audacity. She followed her, relieved that not everyone in the squad was as ice-cold as Isla.

At the stairs, a sob stopped Pearl. She looked around, searching for a faint sniffle. Behind a column, sobbing into her locker, was Ella Hart. The queen of social media was weeping. Her blonde buns trembled with her shoulders. Pearl stared. Aashni groaned.

'What now, Ella? We can't be late.'

02:20.

Ella looked up. Her delicate features were blotchy with crying; a lock of hair had fallen loose.

'They're all ruined. All the new leos from my uncle.' She flung open her locker door.

02:00.

Pearl and Aashni crowded in. On the top shelf of her locker, an open tub of hair gel was lying on its side. Its gooey contents dripped through the slots in the shelf, down on to the leotards hanging below. Pearl pulled one out. It had a giant heart etched out in sparkly crystals. It was also covered in gooey gel. She picked up another, peeling the sticky fabric apart. The delicate heart pattern was gunked up with gel.

'Why didn't you put the lid on, muppet?' said Aashni.

'I was sure I did,' said Ella, her mouth wobbling. 'I don't get it. I like everyone, but someone hates me. Maybe they're jealous that I'm kinda famous. Or of all the presents my uncle sends. It was the same last camp.' Pearl fetched some loo roll from the toilet cubicle.

01:00.

'This'll have to do,' said Pearl, giving one of the leotards a quick wipe down. She handed back a slightly less sticky leotard. Ella put it on, sniffing all the while. Tears hung on her eyelashes like dew. She managed a small smile.

'Oi, enough tears, OK?' said Aashni. 'It's just bad luck. If you seem soft, it makes you a target.'

15

THE INFINITE HANDSTAND

Upside down, the floor gym looked no less impressive than the right way up. The tumble tracks were spotless. The foam pits were brand new. The floor squares were competition-grade. Outside, a breeze shimmered across the lawns, combing the woods beyond. It was a world away from Bagley End Butterflies.

Pearl padded her hands on the plastic matting, shifting her weight. Her toes rested against floor-to-ceiling glass windows. Muscles tensed, she tried to hold herself perfectly straight. Beside her balanced Ryan, glancing at her in a silent 'hello'. Next to him was the rest of the squad. Twelve elite boys and twelve elite girls in a line. All held unfaltering handstands. If Pearl had a hand free, she would have pinched herself.

Miss Cazacu walked along the line. Or rather, she floated along, with a strange, weightless walk. Mrs Lulu followed two steps behind, carrying Miss Cazacu's cup of tea. Two steps behind her trundled a bull of a man. He had the shoulders of a Gruffalo, a round belly, bushy eyebrows and an even bushier moustache. He wore a singlet vest tucked into running shorts that were hitched up too high.

'This year, the International Cup will be greater than ever. Held in Paris, there will be more sponsorship. More media attention. More pressure to bring home gold.' Miss Cazacu's voice was high but fragile. She spoke with an unusual, clipped lilt.

'Am I correct, Mrs Lulu?'

Mrs Lulu nodded.

'Am I correct, Coach Squibb?' The bull of a man nodded deferentially.

'So, the four girls and four boys I select must train harder and perform better than ever. There will be no averageness on my team. The focus will be one hundred per cent on winning the Individual All-Around event. Our sponsors love it because it televises well. I love it because my gymnasts must excel in every event. It will be an excess of excellence.' She paused beside Isla to inspect her position, like she was an insect under a microscope.

'Exemplary posture, Isla.' Then she stopped next to a red-headed boy who looked like a messier, friendlier copy of Isla. 'Lengthen your spine, Hamish, more like your twin . . . No eye-rolling.' She corrected his stance, then floated on.

Pearl's arms ached but she didn't come out of her handstand. Beside her, Ryan held his pose, steady as ever. Pearl wished she could talk to him, but their catch-up would have to wait.

Miss Cazacu paused at Ella, taking in her hair-gel-smeared leotard. 'Presentation is sub-standard. I expect better.' She made a note in her golden notebook. 'Your back is still over-extended, despite all those extra sessions with Coach Squibb.' Coach Squibb mumbled something. Miss Cazacu stopped him with a look.

'Each Saturday, I will score you in a different event. First, floor. Second, bars. Third, vault, with pommel for boys. And finally, beam, with rings for boys. Cup selection will be based on your total score. Be warned, break any rules, you will be sent home. Fail a challenge, you will be sent home. Make excuses, you will be sent home. Six days a week, I expect one hundred per cent effort in your run. Two hundred per cent in conditioning. And three hundred per cent in the skills session. Sauna, ice bath and massage are mandatory, as is your rest day and observing bedtimes. This is not a camp for the mediocre, and excellence comes at a price.' She moved along the line.

'No sloppy ponytails, Aashni. Not a single loose strand of hair. Lose the gum. Also, the scowl. You are Lightning Girl, not Thunder Child . . .'

Pearl glanced across, her shoulders crying out in pain. She sucked her stomach in as Miss Cazacu stopped at the next gymnast. Mo Varma. The boy with the shiny hair and boy-band looks. He glowed with superstar dust. And he was doing a one-handed handstand.

'Ah, Mo, the perfect mix of grit and artistry. It's what makes you our best chance of gold. Don't you agree, Mrs Lulu?' Mrs Lulu nodded, but did not smile. 'I have not seen anything like it since Zoltan Kiss won Olympic gold – back when I was competing myself. Give yourself a clap.' On cue, Mo pushed off his single hand. He did a mid-air clap, before landing on his other hand. Pearl gasped. Miss Cazacu moved closer.

'Spot-on shape too, Jada-Rae,' she said. 'Also a strong chance of success at the Cup.' Jada-Rae nodded, all big eyes and tight braids. Ryan and Pearl shared an eye-roll. Miss Cazacu clearly had her favourites.

At Ryan, Miss Cazacu checked her notebook.

'Ryan Stone, I watched your pommel routine. Excellent

rhythm. Too basic, though.'

She prodded his stomach with her biro. He twitched, eyes narrowing under his elasticated glasses. She frowned. 'Your core strength is above average. Your pain tolerance is not.' She moved on. 'Here, you will learn skills harder than any you've tried before – and more risky.' Ryan shuddered at the word *risky*. 'But these skills are needed for the highest scores. This is what's required to win.' Pearl felt herself shiver at the word *win*. This was everything she had ever wanted, ever. 'When I was a gymnast, I had to sacrifice everything – seeing my parents, holidays, all forms of sugar, music, TV, boyfriends, an education. Everything. But this is how medals are won.'

Miss Cazacu glided along to her. Pearl went rigid. She felt herself being studied. She hoped Miss Cazacu saw her as a lump of clay, ready to be moulded into a champion.

'Ah, our last-minute injury replacement. What would you sacrifice to win?'

Pearl felt herself flush. She hadn't expected a question like this. But she had to answer and prove she was serious.

'Everything, Miss Cazacu,' she puffed, struggling to speak upside down. 'I'm going to win the International Cup,' she added, regretting it before the words left her mouth. She felt eyes turning, noticing her for the first time.

'You are tall. Next year, you may be too tall. Bars will be

a problem. Your feet will trail on the floor.' The honesty hit like a stone. 'You must train hard. The clock is ticking.'

The introduction complete, Miss Cazacu drained her tea and left the gymnasium. She was trailed by Mrs Lulu, then Coach Squibb, two steps behind.

Something sizzled down the line, like a fuse lighting, as the gymnasts flipped down. Pearl rubbed her wrists, thinking. She would surely do anything to become a champion, wouldn't she? It's what Mum would have wanted. Yet somehow the thought frightened her.

16

THE WHITE SPIRIT

The doors on the girls' floor were all open, revealing identical rooms with metal bunk beds. Though the sun was still setting outside, most of the girls were already in their nightwear. Someone was singing. Pearl reached her dorm room, but the door was closed. She knocked. No answer. As she opened the door, Miss Cazacu's words still rang in her mind: *what would you sacrifice to win?*

'Hello?'

The room was narrow but cosy, the uniform layout broken up by a few personal touches. A cheery duvet cover. Fairy lights round the mirror above a small sink. A poster of Elena Cazacu as a young gymnast stuck on the wall. However, that wasn't what made Pearl stand taller. A girl was sitting on the lower bunk in the splits. She wore cheery, floral pyjamas. Eyes closed, earphones in, she tapped her toes to music, humming softly. Pearl gawped, recognizing the girl from the poster in her own bedroom. Jada-Rae Williams. Pearl was sharing a room with Jada-Rae. *The* Jada-Rae. How cool was that? She couldn't wait to tell Max.

Jada-Rae opened her eyes and pulled an earphone out. Pearl caught a snippet of Strauss's 'The Blue Danube' – a routine music classic.

'Hey! Hope you don't mind, I put your case on the top.' Her smile was huge. It appeared like a ray of sunshine, slightly goofy but instantly disarming. 'Is that OK? It's just I like the bottom. Zoe was going to take the top. Until, well . . . her fall.'

'Oh, I don't mind, I like the top,' said Pearl breathlessly. Jada-Rae grinned even more widely. She seemed strong and kind, but totally focused. Her dream gymnast.

As Pearl brushed her teeth, Jada-Rae moved to the floor. She sat cross-legged, tipping a bottle of clear liquid on to a cotton wool pad. A sweet, chemical smell filled the room.

'You were punchy with Miss Cazacu today,' she said, dabbing the pad on the palms of her hands. 'Saying you'll make gold at the Cup.'

'Oh,' said Pearl, flushing. Pressure pumped through her veins.

'Don't worry, she admires ambition. The more outrageous the better.' She gazed at her poster of the young Cazacu. 'Don't be the best. Don't be the best of the best. Be the best of the best of the best,' she imitated Miss Cazacu before cracking up. Her laugh was loud and shameless, bouncing happily around the room. Pearl couldn't help giggling too.

Jada-Rae poured out more clear liquid, then dabbed it on the soles of her feet. Pearl coughed.

'Oh, sorry,' Jada-Rae smiled. She clicked the childproof screw lid of the bottle back on. 'White spirit for hardening my calluses. Have a feel.' Pearl squatted down by Jada-Rae and felt the inside of her hand. Four circles of leather hardness on her palm. Three calluses up each finger. The skin on her thumb was hardened like rhino skin. She glanced at her own hands. The pads were squishy like a baby's.

'Want a go?' said Jada-Rae, standing up. 'I do it morning and night, then I smooth them with an emery board. They're like built-in hand grips. Don't even need to use tape or chalk.' She reached under the blackout curtains to open a window. Pearl shook her head. Mum had always taught her to tape her fingers, use hand grips and coat the apparatus with chalk. She would stick with that.

As Pearl unpacked her suitcase, Jada-Rae stretched and chatted, flooding her with helpful advice on training hard. This was her third camp after all. Pearl placed her folded clothes in the cupboard, catching a whiff of laundry and a reminder of Dad. Home seemed a long way away. She held up her lucky leotard, the hand-sewn plastic pearls making her think of Mum.

'That your competition outfit?' asked Jada-Rae, flipping into a flamingo pose. 'Mrs Lulu will make you a new one. She used to design the outfits for *Strictly Come Dancing*, before she took the job here to be nearer her daughter, so her leos are super-pro. Helps impress the judges.'

'But my mum made me it,' said Pearl, slipping her leotard into the cupboard.

'Fair enough,' said Jada-Rae, looking at her with honest eyes. 'Must be nice having a mum who sews your leos.' She paused before remembering herself. 'I've got to sleep,' she said, turning out the main light. 'The run is at six, but I like to do extra stretching before.'

Pearl was silent as she got into bed. She didn't say that Mum wasn't there any more. The words just wouldn't come out. She couldn't explain that in just three weeks she'd gone from a Covid cough, to chest pains, to being intubated, to it being too late to speak again. All without even a hug goodbye.

The fairy lights glistened against the mirror, throwing a gentle glow into the room. Pearl peered over as she heard the bedside cabinet drawer open. Jada-Rae had taken out a framed photo. Pearl squinted. It was a picture of Jada-Rae with an unusually tall family. They didn't look related. Jada-Rae stroked the frame then put it away. The drawer clicked shut.

Before Pearl had fluffed out her cover, a soft snoring was coming from the bunk below. Pearl closed her eyes. As sleep drifted closer, she wondered if Mum had once been like Jada-Rae, totally focused on competition from dawn until dusk. Could she ever be the same?

Wed 16 Jul

Dad
Hey, Elite Gymnast! How are the cartwheels? Home seems quiet without you. Max asks can he sleep in your room? Love, Dad
07:55

Pearl
Hi Dad. All great here. Everyone seems friendly. Rooming with Jada-Rae Williams! Ryan's with Isla McMorrow's twin. First selection event is floor on Saturday. X
And tell Max he can.
19:57

Dad
Glad it's going well. Remember to enjoy yourself. Keep safe. X
19:58

Pearl
Miss you, Dad. X
20:05

Dad
Miss you too, dumpling. X
20.06

17

THE LONG CLIMB

It was only three days in, yet Pearl was already exhausted. The daily schedule was non-stop: mixed run, breakfast, girls-only conditioning, lunch, girls-only skills, sauna and ice bath, dinner, thirty minutes free time, lights out. Her legs were sore and she'd ripped a blister on both thumbs. However, Pearl knew she had to prove herself, in every exercise of every session.

On the top floor of Leaping Spires, in the ropes and rings gym, the other girls displayed intimidating bendiness. Their hands trickled over their toes and down the flats of their feet, gripping their heels. Pearl dipped further into her seated toe touch, her forefingers gripped around her toes. She pulled her chest down to her aching thighs, wondering how Ryan was getting on in his boys' ice bath session. Above, the glass roof melted into colourless sky, where birds of prey floated on air currents.

Coach Squibb walked around the circle, carrying a plastic crate under one arm. In the classes Miss Cazacu didn't attend, he seemed to find his voice. It was a particularly loud one.

'You know the difference between silver and gold?' His question glinted in the afternoon sunlight. Pearl went to raise her hand, before realizing the question was rhetorical.

'It's the difference between almost-perfection and perfection.' His eyes narrowed under his bushy eyebrows. 'It can be a hundredth of a point. A millisecond. A millimetre. The tiniest of mistakes.' He fished a pair of neoprene cuffs from his crate and threw them at the nearest gymnast. Another pair landed by Pearl's feet.

'How do we reach perfection?' Coach Squibb's moustache quivered. 'Ignore fatigue. Ignore pain. The body can endure far more than the mind thinks.'

Pearl wrinkled her nose. She wasn't sure her mind could tell her aching thighs not to be tired. Her hamstrings grumbled in agreement.

'That's why my challenge is all about endurance,' he

said, putting down the empty crate. He yanked a dangling rope. It must have been fifteen metres to the top, Pearl guessed. Twice as high as their gym back home.

'A seated ascent in pike to the top. Then a descent in straddle position.' He smiled under his moustache. 'Wearing a kilo on each ankle,' he added, pointing at the cuffs he'd handed out. 'That'll separate the kids from the true athletes.'

Pearl slowly strapped the cuffs on, hoping the weakened muscles of her newly recovered ankle would hold. Getting to her weighed-down feet, she made her way to a free rope. It felt like wading through mud. Clutching the rope, she seated herself on the floor and pointed her feet in front, her toes together. The rope seemed to stretch right up into the sky above.

Jada-Rae took the rope beside her.

'Hey, go as fast as you can,' she said, big eyes full of concern. 'Otherwise you'll get the burn. Just don't give up. Not on the way up, not on the way down.' She smiled, full of certainty, then focused on her rope. Pearl nodded, determined to prove herself.

She glanced down the line of gymnasts. There was Ella, her blonde princess buns back to perfect symmetry. Then came Isla, as still as a red-haired robot. Aashni was beyond, in her trademark lightning leotard, scowling at Isla like a wild cat about to spring.

'Let's go,' roared Coach Squibb, clapping his hands together over his belly.

As Pearl lifted off the ground, the stone-like weight of her own body hit her. Arms long, she inched up the rope, legs held out in a right angle to her body, gripping hard. Around her, quiet puffs of effort broke the silence. The floor mats fell away; she climbed higher.

In the edge of her vision, other gymnasts shot up ahead with Ella leading.

'Perfection perfected, Ella,' commented Coach Squibb, his voice softening for once. 'Rest of you are pathetic,' he roared.

By halfway, Pearl's legs began trembling. Her ankle cuffs dragged her downwards. Lactic acid raged in her arms. It was a long way to fall, and getting longer. The burn started in her shoulders, spreading to her wrists. Pain rippled through her. She felt her will crumble. This was way more intense than the ropes at home. She peered down to see the rest of the gymnasts finishing.

'Hurry up, Spare Place,' shouted Coach Squibb. The name echoed across the gymnasium. Pearl swore she heard Isla titter.

Pearl looked up at the glass roof. High above, a bird circled. She gritted her teeth. Blood pumped in her forearms. *You. Can. Do. This.* Hand over stinging hand, she dragged herself up. She tapped the metal fastener at the top. Then every muscle screaming, she butterflied her legs into straddle position. The twisted twine grazed her palms as she descended. Not quite in control, she landed heavily, collapsing on the matting.

Coach Squibb marched over.

'Up you get,' he ordered, towering over her. 'Did I not say? Last one down does five more.' His moustache quivered like a live animal on his lip. 'Or do you not want to be here?'

Pearl set her jaw, thinking of Mum. Of course she wanted to be there. With aching arms she started again. The ankle cuffs felt like lead. But she would not give up. The gymnasts below moved on to the next exercise. She kept going. And going. When she'd finished, her hands were stinging raw and even the birds had flown home to rest.

18

THE CANCELLED PODCAST

In the Hall of Fame, Pearl checked her watch. They only had thirty minutes of free time before bed. This had to cover showering, teeth-brushing, calling home and any other activities. Tonight, this activity was waiting for Ryan to start his podcast. He stood fiddling with his new directional microphone, a present from Gloria for making the squad. Finally, he directed it at Pearl, plugging the jack into his phone.

'OK, recording in three, two, one . . .' Ryan slipped into his podcast voice. This was like his normal voice but more nasal. 'Hi, it's me, Ryan Stone. Welcome back to *Flipping Without Falling*, a gymnastics podcast on how to *train safe and train smart*. Today I'm recording from the Hall of Fame at the National Gymnastics Centre, Leaping Spires. We're standing surrounded by trophies and photos of gymnastic greats. My special guest is GB Mini Elite Squad member, Pearl Bolton.'

'Hi.'

Mrs Lulu entered the hallway from the atrium end, carrying a delivery parcel.

'Welcome to the podcast. This is a particularly special place to be standing, you being the daughter of former GB team gymnast Renshu Chui. Statistically speaking, kids of—' He stopped. 'What?'

Pearl was frowning at him.

'Can you cut that bit about Mum? Don't want everyone knowing. Just adds pressure.' She didn't say, because he should have known already, that it hurt too much to mention her.

'But that's why I thought it would be cool to do the podcast here. There's a photo of her in the GB team.' He beckoned down the hallway, to a faded frame.

Pearl didn't move. She didn't want to look at it. Couldn't.

'Thought you could talk about her experiences here versus yours,' he said. 'I prepared loads of questions.'

'Think up some others.'

They looked round as Mrs Lulu approached. Seeing

Ryan's audio equipment, she began tiptoeing.

'Fine,' said Ryan, returning to Pearl.

'Three, two, one . . . So, Pearl, you've gone from passing your Compulsories a few months ago to being called up last minute for the Mini Elite Squad. A fantastic rise. And now you have a chance to make the International Cup team. How does that make you feel?'

Pearl frowned. She didn't like this question either.

'Makes me feel like I'm going to make the team, then win gold.' She tipped up her chin as she spoke, trying to hide the uncertainty in her voice. She had to believe it. After all, she'd made Mum a promise.

'This is your first experience of an elite training camp. How's it different to training at home?'

Mrs Lulu crept past, trying not to disturb them. She transferred the box under one arm so she could hold her long ponytail to stop it from swishing. Pearl smiled and replied:

'Well, I'd never done an ice bath before. Or so much conditioning. Miss Cazacu's training methods are pretty unusual. Like, she had an exercise where she bangs dustbin lids while we do our routines – to get us used to distractions.'

'I'm sorry to interrupt, poppets,' said a voice as soft as candyfloss.

Ryan paused his recording. Mrs Lulu's pink silk track-suit glowed orange in the evening light.

'You can't publish anything about Miss Cazacu's training methods. What if another team listened to your podcast?' She blinked as though telling them off was hurting her.

'Oh, don't worry, Ryan's podcast only has two followers,' explained Pearl.

Ryan narrowed his eyes under his glasses.

'A few followers,' Pearl corrected herself.

'Still. She'd have you kicked off the squad if she knew. And she wouldn't like you talking about anyone's routines, any new moves or her approach to rest and recovery either.' Mrs Lulu smiled. Her blue eyes softened in sympathy.

Ryan rubbed the back of his neck, thinking. 'That doesn't leave much. Maybe the injury rate here?'

'Sponsors wouldn't take kindly to that at all.'

'The curse of Leaping Spires?'

Miss Lulu put her box down, looking shocked. She took Ryan firmly by the shoulders.

'That kind of talk would upset a lot of the staff and frighten the gymnasts. It won't make you many friends. I'm not trying to ruin your podcast, but honestly, I wouldn't go there. Maybe you could talk about the dazzling architecture of Leaping Spires? The lovely fruit trees in the atrium?'

Ryan looked unimpressed.

'How about your favourite Fruitogade flavour?'

Ryan looked even more unimpressed.

Mrs Lulu gave him a kindly pat on the shoulder and made to leave.

'Oops, almost forgot!' She bent down and picked up the box. 'Miss Cazacu's notebook delivery. She gets through them at such a rate!'

Pearl and Ryan watched after her as she walked away, ponytail bouncing behind her. Down the hallway, she paused. Gazing at the photos, she sighed sadly. From under the collar of her tracksuit, she pulled a locket necklace. She pressed it to her lips and then dropped it back under her collar. She noticed them watching.

'How about a podcast about some of the lesser-known gymnastic greats?' she offered. 'You could start with my daughter, Allegra Sweet. Such talent, though no one remembers her nowadays.' Ryan shook his head. Giving up, she swung away through the double doors.

'Well, that's my podcast wrecked,' said Ryan, as they walked glumly back to their dorms. 'Total waste of my new mic. You know it can pick up sound thirty metres away.'

'Maybe this is a good thing,' said Pearl, trying to cheer him up. 'Less distraction for our first assessment?'

'Why are you always so positive?' said Ryan, rolling his eyes.

'Why are you always so negative?' Pearl replied with a grin. Ryan couldn't help but laugh.

19

THE TINKLING TAMBOURINE

In the floor gym, the gymnasts finished their afternoon warm-up. Pearl sat back on her shins, rubbing her biceps. One more day until the first of the four assessments. All she or any of the gymnasts could think about was walkovers, handsprings and landings.

'What is a tumbler's greatest enemy?' asked Miss Cazacu. She stood at the end of a tumble track, swaying lightly on the springy surface. All the gymnasts sat a little straighter as she looked at them. Coach Squibb balanced on a ladder, leaning over the foam pit. He threaded what looked like a tambourine along a high wire. It dangled high above the pool of foam blocks, twisting gently.

'Gravity,' Miss Cazacu answered. Pearl bit her lip nervously. Whatever the exercise, this time she had to succeed.

'In today's challenge you will triumph over gravity.' She pointed up at the suspended tambourine. 'You must touch one of these as you tumble. With your hands, your feet, your nose, whatever. As long as you get the height.'

The gymnasts lined up, waiting their turn. Pearl stood near the back, drumming her fingers together nervously. Aashni went first. She pounded down the tumble track, handsprung down and bounced up like elastic. She flew through the air, flipping up fearlessly, catching the tambourine with a bang. She landed in the foam pit with a whoop. No wonder she was an unbeatable tumbler. Pearl watched on as each gymnast did their run-up. Time and time again the tambourine trilled. Even Ella, who had been on the loo since breakfast with a stomach upset, succeeded.

Reaching the front of the queue, Jada-Rae turned back.

'Only way to make it is a double front-handspring layout. You can do it!' She saluted and began her perfect run-up before throwing herself forward. She bounced into one handspring, a second, then soared upwards, flipping over. The tambourine crashed in applause. She landed elegantly in the foam pit. Miss Cazacu's face almost broke a smile.

Pearl saluted, heart heavy as stone. Big tumbles weren't her speciality. Too many flips gave her the twisties – that sickening feeling where up and down got lost. And she'd never done a double front-handspring layout before. However, Miss Cazacu was judging, so she had to perform.

With a deep inhale, she started sprinting. Counting her steps. Knees high. Leaning forward. Elbows pummelling. The foam pit approached. Arms circling backwards, she launched into a handspring. And another, trying to gain height. She straightened into a layout, tipping forward. Time slowed as she spun. She felt something brush her toes. The tambourine trembled, tinkling lightly. She tumbled back round, flopping into the foam pit. She had done it! Only just, but it was still a sound! And she'd done her first double front-handspring layout. On a tumble track and into a foam pit, but still.

'Much to work on,' nodded Miss Cazacu. 'But this was not a total disaster. I have hope. Join the others.'

Pearl moved with the other gymnasts to the conditioning exercise, a gentle one hundred front levers. As she joined them, Miss Cazacu gave her the tiniest nod. As if she had, with that reckless leap upside down, landed in the world of the Elites. Teetering right on the edge of it, but in, nonetheless.

20

THE GREEN MUFFIN

Pearl still hadn't got used to the slickness of the canteen. With white, shiny surfaces, wipe-clean walls and chrome edgings, it seemed more designed for astronauts than kids. She half-expected a rocket to launch from behind the serving hatch. A motivational poster read: *Eat clean to get lean*. Ryan was in the lunch queue. With their new schedules, mealtimes were the only time they saw each other.

'What's up?' she said as they neared the serving hatch.

'Other than the total lack of anything sugary?' said Ryan, scanning the food choices. They were all very . . . green. Pearl wasn't really a fan of eating anything green.

Green was not a colour she associated with fun food. Pizza wasn't green. Sausage rolls were never green. Spaghetti bolognese definitely wasn't green. In fact the only greens she liked in food were the pickle in Big Macs and mint chocolate chip ice cream.

'And not being allowed a sip of Fruitogade when they're sponsoring everything?'

Pearl's stomach gurgled in disapproval. She loved Fruitogade after all.

'And Mum's fruit cake getting confiscated while Ella gets special food deliveries from her uncle?' He nodded over at where Ella sat nibbling a single green muffin from a Tupperware box.

'She has special dispensation because she keeps getting tummy upsets at camp,' shrugged Pearl, picking out the celery soup.

'And the endless conditioning?' He picked up a beet-root burger with a sigh. 'I did one thousand combined pike-ups, chin-ups and leg lifts this morning. You know, seventy per cent of injuries are from over-training?' Pearl never got stiff normally. However, after sitting in over-splits for half the morning, muscles in her hips ached that she hadn't known she had. She wasn't going to tell Ryan that, though.

'And Coach Squibb calling me the Nursery Section?

Just because I won't add a double layout into my floor routine? And he calls Hamish the Lesser Twin.'

'Calls me Spare Place.' Pearl picked up a spinach frittata too. Whatever a frittata was.

'I don't like it.'

As Ryan rattled off a statistic about gymnastic injuries, Pearl wound round the tables. She gazed over at the unofficial top table. Jada-Rae sat laughing at Mo's jokes. Aashni and Isla were steadily ignoring each other. Ella wiped away green crumbs before taking a selfie. Pearl wondered if she'd ever get to sit with them.

Ryan continued, undeterred:

'Pearl – are you even listening?'

Pearl sat down at an empty table at the back.

'I'm trying to have a Positive Mental Attitude. And so should you.'

Ryan banged his tray down with a clatter.

'I want to make it here just as much as you do. I just don't like being pushed into moves I'm not ready for – it's the fastest way to get injured. This place has a reputation for injuries. You know they talk about the curse of Leaping Spires?'

'Now you're being paranoid,' said Pearl weakly. She tried a spoonful of celery soup. It tasted like washing-up water.

'Am I? Did you hear what happened to the girl whose place you got?' Pearl frowned, not wanting to be reminded she was the spare.

'Shattered vertebrae. I found out she fell from the ropes on settling-in day. Honestly, there's something creepy going on here. It's not right.'

'Jada-Rae doesn't believe in the curse,' Pearl said sharply. 'She says when everyone's pushing themselves to their limit, injuries happen. Gymnastics is tough, it's just part of the deal.'

Ryan went quiet. They listened to the clatter of crockery and the scraping of stackable chairs in silence. Pearl wished she hadn't said anything. When Hamish plonked his tray down, grumbling about his sister teasing him, they both felt relieved. Slowly, they relaxed. And Pearl decided to forget about curses and injuries, despite Ryan's warnings.

21

THE LAST SLOT

It was a beautiful morning. Sunlight sparkled through the huge glass panes of the floor gym, turning the chalk in the air to glitter. However, no one seemed to notice because it was Saturday. The first assessment. The floor exercise, where for ninety seconds, in twelve metres squared of sprung flooring, gymnasts would give elegance to strength and artistry to power. On the far side of the gym, the boys' event was coming to a close, overseen by Coach Squibb.

Stretching on the mats, Pearl pushed her face into her shins. She was wearing her lucky leotard, but nerves jangled through her. She walked through her routine in her mind. She tried to think positive thoughts: Welsh skies, Gloria's kitchen, playing football with Max, Dad's belly-laugh. Anything to take away the quivering in her stomach.

'Today each of you will perform your full floor routine,' said Miss Cazacu. She stood on a foam block with her golden notebook.

Jada-Rae sat beside her in the splits, drinking in Miss Cazacu's words. There was a toughness in her chin, like a soldier going into battle. Pearl set her chin too.

'I will assess both difficulty level and execution,' continued Miss Cazacu, rocking on to tiptoes in her trainers. 'Just as the judges will in the Cup. You will go in current rank order. First up, Jada-Rae.'

In the corner, Mrs Lulu began the music. Strauss's 'The Blue Danube'. Pearl stretched out muscles that refused to untense, watching Jada-Rae. The first notes unfurled; she pirouetted into action. She twisted and spun to the melody, her hands and feet beating out the waltz. She soared up with the violins; she somersaulted down with the cellos. To the woodwind's flutter she flipped and sprang. As the orchestra swelled, her tumbles reached a crescendo. She was a masterpiece, her acrobatics in perfect harmony. The final notes died away and Jada-Rae returned to herself. She sat down, stretching out on the mats like she was sunbathing.

'Twelve point five. Next up, Isla,' said Miss Cazacu, scribbling in her notebook. Jada-Rae copied down a note in her own tiny, white notebook too.

Pearl felt anxious all over. Jada-Rae's score was huge. How could she compete? She watched nervously as Isla chalked up her hands, presented and began. She moved like a well-oiled machine, if a well-oiled machine could tumble to a Bach concerto. Every jump, every twist and every somersault was executed with pinpoint accuracy. Every line was sharp; every extension was crisp. It was as if she was guided by an invisible algorithm. Until something misaligned and her final handsprings floundered. She finished, arms raised, face full of disappointment.

'My hands went suddenly itchy,' she complained, stepping back to the mats.

'So says the Whinger,' growled Coach Squibb, coming to sit by Miss Cazacu.

'No need for the name-calling, Coach Squibb,' tutted Miss Cazacu. 'But it is true, excuses are a distraction. And champions do not make excuses, Isla. Ten point four.'

Pearl's mouth went dry. Isla was a star gymnast and even she was struggling with the pressure.

As the other gymnasts performed their routines, Pearl's throat tightened. Ella, in a shiny new leotard from her uncle, dazzled to a waltz. Twelve point one. However, it was Aashni who crept into the lead with a tempest of tumbles to a rock track, scoring twelve point six. They all seemed so advanced, nailing moves she'd never even tried before. She felt like a duckling among eagles, there to fill the last slot. She shook out her limbs. It was her turn.

'And finally, Zoe . . .' Miss Cazacu paused, crossed something out in her notebook. 'My mistake, and finally, Pearl.'

Pearl made her way over to the blue square of sprung flooring, shoulders stiff with tension.

'Hey.'

Pearl looked round. Ryan had jogged over, ignoring Miss Cazacu's disapproving tut.

'You can do this,' he said, holding out his fist. They did their exploding fist bump. For the first time, Pearl felt embarrassed by their superstition.

'Thanks,' she blushed, feeling everyone looking. 'And well done on your routine.'

She cricked her neck and made a salute. This was her moment. It had to be. The first notes of 'Overture from the Barber of Seville' kicked in. She was off. As the familiar melody kicked in, everything else fell away. She danced and twisted, the moves worn smooth from hours of practice. Her limbs moved fluidly as the tempo picked up. She split-leapt up then went straight into a handspring, her body made of symmetry. A step and a simple pivot into the corner. She inhaled, channelling her nerves for her tumble sequence. The overture reached its crescendo as she launched into her aerials. She flipped and dived and soared. She finished, arms raised, fingers flexed, just like Mum had taught her. She looked over at Miss Cazacu, every muscle straining for her reaction.

'Ten point nine,' noted Miss Cazacu, stepping off her foam block. 'Putting you fifth place in the rankings,' she said. 'Execution was perfection. But difficulty levels were average and the outfit is ordinary. Room for improvement. Train hard. Don't rely on luck. Cup team is not impossible from here.'

Pearl couldn't hide her smile. She wasn't last, or even second last. She was one place off the team. And she was going to train harder than Miss Cazacu could even imagine.

22

THE TWO BRANCHES

It was Sunday, the one rest day and the one lie-in of the week. However, rather than staying curled up under the duvet, Pearl and Jada-Rae had dressed in the dark. They were sneaking out because Jada-Rae had extra training to do. And now Pearl had a chance of making the Cup team, she was going too.

In silence, they slipped down the stairs. The canteen was quiet as they tiptoed to the back exit. No one was up yet, not even the kitchen staff.

'What if we get caught?' asked Pearl, pulse racing as they crossed the car park. The first rays of morning edged over the tops of the trees.

'We won't,' grinned Jada-Rae. 'Trust me. This is the one place no one will see us. Last camp Zoe and I went here every Sunday.'

On the far side of the car park, a path led down a row of Staff Only maisonettes. Two low storeys of concrete made up the row of identical apartments, all with matching black front doors. Jada-Rae crept along the path, darting from the cover of one wheelie bin to another. Pearl joined her. She raised her head, meerkat-like.

'Coach Squibb's up early.'

They watched him a moment, bustling about in his kitchen with an apron on. He weighed out nuts and seeds into a bowl, then greased a tray.

They moved on. As they reached the end of the buildings they broke into a run. Pearl chased Jada-Rae across the lawns, towards the lake, making footprints in the dew. They pulled up by the shore, laughing. A faint mist still lingered over the lake.

'And how exactly is this bars training?' said Pearl. It was only seven days until the bars assessment, and she needed to make every moment count.

'You'll see,' said Jada-Rae, striding ahead. They walked round the bank towards a giant willow tree. It leant over the lake, fronds fluttering over the water. She slipped through a curtain of leaves. Pearl looked over her shoulder.

The glass roof of Leaping Spires glinted in the distance, just out of shouting range. It worried her to be breaking rules, but Jada-Rae had the confidence of a champion, and it was hard to say no.

Pearl parted the drooping branches and stepped under the canopy. Inside was like a secret, green cathedral. A huge trunk twisted up to the sky. Over the lake, a pair of perfectly horizontal smooth branches stretched out. One was higher than the other, spaced a gymnastic leap apart. Jada-Rae kicked off her trainers and stripped down to her leotard.

'Seriously?' laughed Pearl, stripping down too.

'Hey, Miss Cazacu wasn't wrong about your outfit,' said Jada-Rae. 'Mrs Lulu would knock you up an amazing one.' Pearl looked down. She'd put on her lucky leotard by mistake in the dark. 'I know your mum made it, but it won't help you win. She'd understand, wouldn't she?' Jada-Rae started climbing the gnarled trunk.

Pearl watched Jada-Rae as she leant across and swung up on to the lower branch. She landed surely, the balls of her feet steadying the slight sway.

'Your mum's not around any more, is she?' Jada-Rae said as she tiptoed along the branch. Pearl didn't answer, stunned. 'Mine neither.'

Jada-Rae stood over the water – silent, still and small.

For a moment she wasn't the great Jada-Rae Williams, Olympic hopeful, just a young girl with a big heart and only herself to lean on. She gripped the branch and swung into a giant, her toes skimming centimetres above the water. She spun up into a handstand. Turned around, an upstart and a release. Pearl gasped as Jada-Rae flew across, catching the higher branch.

'She told me to light up the world with my shine, and that's what I'm going to do,' Pearl said. Jada-Rae spun and flew between the two branches. Pearl felt strangely safe, like she could tell her new friend anything. Things she'd never even talked about with Ryan.

'I sort of thought, if I do, it'll make her proud. Make some sense of losing her,' she said, the words tumbling out.

Jada-Rae soared up into full-out, splashing down into the lake. She yelled happily, then did an excellent dolphin imitation. As if the water wasn't cold at all. Shaking the water out of her eyes, she swam to the side.

'I can help you make her proud,' said Jada-Rae. She looked at her with big, honest eyes. 'Your turn.'

Pearl climbed up, feeling strangely fearless. Balancing along the branch, she moved into position. The water rippled below. Deep breath. If Jada-Rae could do it, so could she. She dipped down and clutched the branch. It was smooth and the perfect size for a hand grip. She was glad she'd given in to white-spiriting her hands.

Pearl swung into her routine, rising and falling between the two branches. Maybe it was the glow of the leaves as the sun steadily rose behind. Maybe it was the cocooning from the breeze. Maybe it was the gentle lap of water. Maybe it was because she'd finally said what she'd been thinking a long time. But the space felt secure enough that when Jada-Rae suggested trying a full-out, Pearl didn't even hesitate.

Twisting.

Spinning.

Splashing.

The shock of cold robbed her lungs of air. Every muscle contracted. Her skin seized up. It was like a bath of icicles. Jada-Rae cheered. Pearl yelled and beat the water with her fist. She had done it. She could do it. She was going to do it again and again and again. By the time they'd finished their practice, Pearl was a mass of goosepimples and chattering teeth. Her fingers and toes had a blueish tinge. She didn't care, though, because this was the way to make the Cup team.

23

THE HIGHEST SEAT

The walk back from the lake had chilled Pearl, especially as they hadn't taken towels. She was dizzy with cold, like her head was made of ice cream. Her hands were numb; she wasn't sure if this was the start of hypothermia.

'Are you sure this is a good idea?' she said uncertainly. She didn't know if they were allowed into the Rest and Recovery Centre without adult supervision. It was a large, tiled room full of hard edges and the smell of antiseptic. One side was lined with three giant raised baths with temperature gauges, each ten degrees cooler than the last. On the other side were three saunas of increasing temperatures. Normally it was filled with red-faced gymnasts in towels, and the slapping of wet feet. However, during breakfast slot on a Sunday morning it was deathly quiet. The massage beds lay empty, clean paper covers freshly laid out on them.

'The more you cool down and heat up your muscles, the quicker you recover, the harder you can train. It's basic science,' shrugged Jada-Rae, heading for the furthest sauna. The one with the temperature gauge which read eighty degrees. The one with the sign reading: *Over 13s only.*

'You want to make the Cup team or what?' She grinned and slipped in.

Pearl followed. Inside was a small, dark space, with walls lined with wood. Three tiered wooden benches circled a stove. The heat hit her like a sandstorm. Her throat scratched. Jada-Rae clambered up on to the top bench and leant back on the wooden boards as if sunbathing. Pearl sat on the lowest tier of seating. Slowly, the heat expanded through her. She felt like she was thawing. The ends of her fingers throbbed and then stung, as they turned from icicles to rods of fire.

'Think I should get out, really hurts.'

'Just stick with it,' said Jada-Rae chirpily. 'Your muscles will feel good as new after. Then we can work on our handstands in our room.' Her unwavering positivity gave Pearl a boost of confidence. However, her toes were tingling unpleasantly and the throbbing had spread to her head.

'Ryan always says pain is a signal you should stop.'

'Ryan isn't going to help you get selected,' replied Jada-Rae. The logic was hard to argue with. 'So the older Elites do two minutes in here, but we'll do double. Agree?'

Pearl hesitated, unsure. Her head hurt, as did her throat. However, there was no disagreeing with Jada-Rae's invincible optimism. She watched the clock on the wall as sweat dripped down her forehead. Four minutes felt like a long time.

'Hey, try this seat,' offered Jada-Rae. 'Hotter up here.' Pearl felt herself stumbling up to the top bench. The heat was even more aggressive. It got worse when Jada-Rae poured a ladleful of water on the stove's hot coals. However, if Pearl wanted to get selected she had to stay.

All of a sudden, the floor began to swim. Actually, everything began to swim. And spin. She was fainting and falling. In and out of consciousness. The last thing Pearl remembered was a rosy-cheeked medic carrying her out, complaining loudly about gymnasts not knowing where to draw the line.

24

THE EXTRA PACKET

Pearl came to on a trolley bed. A hospital-issue blue curtain had been pulled around it. Heat, cold and the nagging feeling she was in trouble washed over her. Her head swam. On a side table lay a tray of medical supplies, neatly laid out – zinc oxide tape, surgical scissors, scalpels, spare blades and dressings.

'Good you came to fetch me so quickly,' came the medic's measured tone behind the curtain. 'Could have been very dangerous otherwise.' It was the doctor from the trials. The one who thought there was more to gymnastics than scores.

'That's OK, Dr Pond. Hey, what are friends for?' replied

Jada-Rae. Despite feeling sick, Pearl smiled.

'Now I'll prescribe you another packet for your back pain, but you must stop losing them, OK?'

Pearl sat up gingerly, feeling dizzy. Through a gap in the curtain, she could see into the room. It was like a pharmacy mixed with a doctor's surgery, complete with anatomical posters, an outdated computer and a full-size skeleton on wheels. Dr Pond had her back to her, unlocking a glass medicine cabinet. Jada-Rae stood hopping from foot to foot. Pearl felt like jumping up to give her a hug. Her friend, her secret extra-training coach and now her life-saver. But suddenly the wooziness took over and she retched.

Dr Pond pulled back Pearl's curtain at speed, her well-scrubbed cheeks flushing.

'Off you go, Jada-Rae.' She thrust a sick bowl in Pearl's face. 'I won't mention anything to your coaches, if you insist,' she called as the door swung to. Once Pearl had finished dry-retching, she looked up. Dr Pond had pulled up a chair next to the bed. She brushed a speck of dust off another pair of brand-new, snow-white sneakers.

'I understand why Elites over-train,' she said, handing Pearl a plastic cup of fizzy orange liquid. 'There's a lot of pressure. From coaches, parents.' Pearl tasted the drink. Sugar rushed through her, clearing her grogginess.

Super-sweet and sickly; she recognized the taste. Fruitogade. Every vending machine at Leaping Spires was full of it. However, only staff had the necessary swipecard.

'The window to be a top gymnast is so small and it's a race against time.' She looked at her seriously, her grey eyes unblinking. Pearl took another sip.

'But if you over-train, and aren't sensible about your recovery, it can be dangerous. Career-ending. Life-threatening, even.'

Pearl stared hard at her cup. Her muscles actually felt OK, so perhaps it had been worth it, despite the nausea. Dr Pond sighed.

'You've heard of the Curse of Leaping Spires?' she said. Pearl's eyes widened. Dr Pond pointed up at the bowing shelf above her desk. 'Look at those.'

Pearl stepped down off the trolley bed. She steadied herself, still feeling light-headed. There was a row of lever arch files on the shelf, each neatly labelled: *Injuries*.

'There are so many, I have to start a new file every month. The curse? It's not knowing when ambition stops being good for you.' Her walkie-talkie crackled into life:

'Dr Pond. Injury in the stairwell.'

'Not another,' said Dr Pond, shaking her head. She hurried out of the room. Pearl downed the Fruitogade, studying the files as she did so. She bit her lip, remembering how long her last injury took to heal. Was pushing yourself to the brink of injury ever worth it? What if that's what it took to win gold?

25

THE ORANGE SPILL

By the time Pearl reached the stairwell, a crowd had gathered. They clustered around the foot of the banisters. Gymnasts leant over the top, looking down with grave faces.

Pearl craned around the tops of heads. The twins' red hair and Ryan's spiky hair were right in the way.

'Who is it?' said Pearl, straining to see.

'Can't tell,' said Jada-Rae, squatting down to see between the forest of legs. 'Hey, you feeling better?'

Pearl nodded uncertainly.

Mrs Lulu bobbed to the front, parting the crowd.

'The poor poppet,' she gasped, squeezing back out.

'I must find Miss Cazacu, she'll be devastated. Coach Squibb!' Pearl glanced behind her. Down the hallway of trophies, Coach Squibb was stomping away. 'Coach Squibb!'

Pearl slipped forward. Finally, she saw. At the foot of the banisters was Mo. Right where he normally landed his signature banister slide. He lay on his back, eyes shut, out cold below the sign that read: *No handstands. No cartwheels. No backflips*. Around him, a puddle of orange, sticky liquid slicked the tiled floor.

Dr Pond stepped gingerly through the orange spill, trying not to dirty her fancy trainers. She knelt beside him, checking for breathing. She held up his arm, taking his pulse. The crowd tensed. Aashni crossed her arms tighter; Ella wept harder. Jada-Rae gripped Pearl's hand. A single tear rolled down her cheek.

Mo reared up in an intake of breath and a swish of shiny hair. The crowd untensed. Their most popular gymnast would be OK. Dr Pond caught him as he flopped back down.

'Give him some space,' said Dr Pond calmly. 'Let's get you to the medical bay. Check you out for concussion.' As Mo went to get up, he clutched his knee in pain.

'And a knee injury,' sighed Dr Pond. As she helped move her new patient away in the direction of Rest and

Recovery, Pearl realized she was shaking.

The crowd of gymnasts cleared, their voices hushed. For once no one was doing an impromptu handstand or cartwheel. Ryan moved to Pearl's side.

'You OK? You look pale.'

'Never been better.' Pearl decided not to mention the episode in the sauna. Up on the stairs, Jada-Rae motioned at Pearl to join her for extra stretching in their room. Pearl shook her head, feeling a strange tugging between her newest friend and her oldest. As Jada-Rae moved out of sight, Ryan's frown thickened.

'Seen you with her a lot.'

'Of course, she's my roomie.' Pearl felt defensive, she wasn't sure why. 'You hang out with Hamish.'

'Only because you're never about.'

They reverted to silence, staring at the spot where Mo had landed. Ryan looked up at the banisters, then back at the orange puddle. He bent down and put a finger to the liquid. He tasted it.

'Fruitogade,' he said quietly. 'So weird it's spilt right here when I've never seen a single gymnast drinking the stuff. Kind of suspicious. Especially as only the staff have access to the vending machine.'

'Maybe one of the staff spilt it?' Pearl suggested.

'Or maybe it wasn't an accident?' Ryan replied.

Pearl shook her head. It was an accident, just a really unlucky accident. For the rest of the day, she tried to focus on other things. Like perfecting her bars routine for Saturday's assessment. However, as murmurs of the curse of Leaping Spires played on everyone's lips, she couldn't help but wonder.

Wed 23 Jul

Dad

How's your week going, dumpling? Haven't heard from you much.

19:45

Thu 24 Jul

Dad

All OK? Max got a new goal. Gloria's been bringing me over apple crumble.

12:01

Pearl

Sorry, Dad, so busy. It's bars this week. Lots to work on with my routine.

19:50

Dad

Good to hear from you! Finally! Enjoying yourself? How's Ryan? Gloria worries about him. You know what she's like.

19:51

Pearl

Boys training separately from us, so not seeing him much. He came 5th like me in his first test. And I'm mainly hanging with Jada-Rae when we do have free time. (Which is never!) She's helping me loads on my routine, though.

19:52

Dad

Well, don't forget your old pal. He's been good to you.

19:55

Fri 25 Jul

Pearl

Sorry, it was lights out. Then not allowed to message in the day.

19:45

Dad

Remember to rest up.

19:46

Pearl

Yeah, right! No time for that. Our next test is tomorrow. Wish me luck.

19:46

Dad

Good luck and keep safe. X

19:47

Pearl

Did Mum like Leaping Spires?

22:51

Dad

You should be sleeping! She said it was the making of her. Sweet dreams.

22:52

26

THE TEAM PHOTO

In the bars gym, rain drummed on glass. It scattered mottled shadows over the high bars, the low bars and the wires that held them taut. The squad stretched, silently preparing. Today was the second assessment: uneven bars for the girls with Miss Cazacu, parallel bars for the boys with Coach Squibb, performing in rank order.

Pearl watched the first four routines nervously, assessing every error, counting difficulty levels in her head. She noted Jada-Rae's extra half-step on her dismount. She suspected Aashni had a tenth of a point deducted for frowning. She saw Ella's transitions falter a touch. Then she was up.

If she was going to perform in any of the assessments, it was this one. Bars was her strongest event, after all. She stood up, shaking out her limbs. Jada-Rae raised a hand. Pearl high-fived her and made her way over to the uneven bars. Incredibly, her muscles felt OK. Jada-Rae's methods might cause near frostbite, fainting and a throbbing headache. However, it definitely felt to Pearl like they worked. She felt strong – ready to perform. The bars leered at her from the other end. Pearl cricked her neck and saluted. As she looked at her fellow gymnasts, for the first time she noticed something in their eyes. Were they willing her to fall?

She stepped on the springboard and leapt up. Not thinking of anything but catching and releasing bars. An upstart, then up on to the high bar into handstand. She began to flow, wrists strong, hips following arms. Her body drew lines in the air. A full breath before her newest move: a forward giant followed by a backwards straddle roll. Without Gloria there to suggest it was too tricky, she had put it in her routine. As well as dismounting with a full-out, inspired by Jada-Rae.

She spun a full circle round the bar, body extended, and released. Mid-air she straddled her legs, rolling backwards while moving forward. With perfect timing she caught the bar. Up back to the high bar and into her full-out. The ground reared up as she landed. Her knees buckled to hold her weight but she didn't take a step. Not backwards, not forwards. She took a half-second to shore herself up before straightening into a salute.

A staccato clapping sound echoed across the gym. Pearl looked behind her. Miss Cazacu had put her golden notebook under her arm and was clapping. The edges of her lips were turned upwards in what might be described as a smile.

'There is gold dust there, as I predicted,' she said. 'Thirteen point one, putting you in the lead in today's assessment. For a first-timer at camp, this is impressive.'

Pearl's heart swelled, pushing against her ribcage. This was more than she could have dreamt of.

'Wow,' gasped Jada-Rae, 'that puts you fourth overall in the rankings, in line to make the Cup team . . . unless Isla tops your score.'

The other gymnasts rushed over to congratulate her, like bees drawn to honey. Ella seemed genuinely happy for her, despite the pressure of having a new contender for the team.

'Our new star on bars,' she giggled. 'Can I take a photo of Pearl with everyone, Miss Cazacu? So I can introduce her to my followers. Please?'

'OK, just this once,' agreed Miss Cazacu, pausing to take

a cup of tea from Mrs Lulu.

Pearl puffed with pride as Ella waved everyone into place around the bars. Coach Squibb, with unusual jollity, paused the boys' event to let the boys join in. Ryan leant awkwardly against the bar frame. Hamish draped a cheery arm over his shoulder. Dr Pond was roped in. Even Miss Cazacu stood stiffly at the edge. Only Isla didn't. She chalked her hands in the chalk bowl, waiting for the bars to clear.

'High praise from Miss Cazacu,' she said icily to Pearl as they passed. 'We'd best watch out for you.'

27

THE SILVER GLINT

Team photo over, the bar cleared. Pearl was still buzzing with all the compliments as a hush fell. The final competitor was on. Isla strode up to the bar, stern-faced. Would she achieve a performance that knocked Pearl off her new-found Cup team spot? Pearl walked to the back of the gymnasium and sat on a pile of mats. She didn't wish ill on any gymnast, yet she ached to hang on to that winning feeling.

Despite herself, she looked across. Isla was spinning, stretching and straddling on the bars. Every second of her sequence was perfectly timed. All building to her highest-difficulty move. The pinnacle of her routine. Perfectly executed, it could catapult her past Pearl in the rankings. Pearl couldn't watch, but neither could she look away.

Knees tight, Isla flipped up, spinning high. Descending, she reached for the bar, thumbs touching. She caught it squarely. It was spectacular, until she screamed. Shrill and pained. She ripped her hands from the bar, pulling them tight to her chest as she fell. With a crack of bone, she landed. There was a tick of realization, before everyone rushed to her side.

Dr Pond was there first. She spoke into her walkie-talkie. An ambulance was being called. Coach Squibb rushed over, belly swaying, leaving his group, which he never did. Miss Cazacu crouched down, whispering questions in Dr Pond's ear. All the girls and boys crowded round.

'This is proper bad,' muttered Aashni, arms crossed.

'It's the curse,' whispered Ella, eyes full of tears.

'She didn't even fall that far,' was all Pearl could mumble.

Pearl backed away. Jada-Rae sat by the chalk stand, head in hands. Was she crying? Pearl thought of going to comfort her. Didn't. Couldn't. This was all too much. She watched as two paramedics entered, already wheeling a stretcher trolley. They knelt down. Then a careful lift. Isla's eyes widened in pain, but she wasn't speaking. A drop of blood dripped on to the mats.

'Assessments are finished for today,' announced Miss Cazacu. 'You may do free practice.'

However, everyone followed the stretcher down the spiral stairs, like a funeral march. Except Pearl. A nausea spread inside her, growing with each snatched inhale. That scream. Why scream *after* catching the bar?

In the empty gymnasium, she tiptoed back over to the uneven bars. She looked up and focused, then refocused. Because there, under the high bar, in the dead centre, was something that made her blood slow to a crawl. Right in the middle, on the underside, was the strangest thing. It was silvery and sharp-edged. Disturbed, she mounted the lower bar. Carefully, she swung and caught the high bar, to the very left. She shifted along, moving upside down like a sloth. There it was. A paper-thin blade was taped lengthwise with zinc oxide tape, so the sharp cutting edge stuck out. It was enough to make a gymnast recoil, but not to be noticeable.

Pearl dropped down, heart gripped tight. This was no curse. It was much worse. It was proof that the accidents were anything but accidents, and that somebody would stop at nothing to injure the star gymnasts.

28

THE CURSE OF LEAPING SPIRES

The ambulance circled round the forecourt, its blue lights reflecting in the puddles. The rain had intensified. Pearl wove around the assembled kids and staff. They watched grimly, getting sodden.

One of them must have done this. Someone was responsible. Pearl gazed at them. Coach Squibb, shaking his head. Miss Cazacu, stone-faced. Dr Pond, stepping round a puddle in her box-fresh trainers. Mrs Lulu, blowing her nose into a tissue. Hamish, eyes cast down. Jada-Rae, Ella and Aashni, linking arms.

Ryan stood away from them, shoulders hunched, looking wet and miserable. The last thing Pearl wanted to do was show him what was taped to the bar, yet he was the only person she could truly trust.

The ambulance sped off down the drive. The crowd slowly dispersed. Pearl tapped Ryan on the arm.

'It wasn't an accident,' she whispered. 'Follow me.'

They slipped back through the atrium. Gymnasts from the older groups were huddled in groups, whispering. Staff spoke in low voices. Even the fruit trees seemed to mutter as they passed them. They climbed the spiral staircase back up to the bars gymnasium.

'You think it's the curse?' said Ryan as they hurried across the mats.

'I don't think there's a curse, I think someone is causing this.'

'You mean, like sabotage?' asked Ryan.

'Sabo-what?'

They stopped under the uneven bars.

'It's when someone destroys stuff on purpose,' he said.

'Does this count?' Pearl pointed to the underside of the bars.

Ryan looked up. Squinted. Took his elasticated glasses off and cleaned them. Snapped them back in place. Stared again. Then eyeballed Pearl, confused. Pearl looked up. Her jaw dropped.

The strip of tape and the scalpel blade were gone.

'But . . . it was there a moment ago!' Pearl checked the other side of the bars. Nothing. 'There was a little blade taped down.' She inspected the mats. Nothing.

Ryan looked at her, eyebrows raised. Admittedly, it seemed a little ridiculous now.

'You believe me, don't you?' asked Pearl as they retraced their steps across the gym.

Ryan paused at the top of the spiral staircase, staring out across the atrium. He ran his fingers through his spiky hair. Pearl bit her lip.

'You're my friend, 'course I believe you,' he said, turning down the stairs. 'What kind of blade was it?'

'A scalpel blade, like you see in the medical room.' Pearl jogged after him, spiralling down.

'What kind of tape?'

Below, the lunch bell sounded. Gymnasts streamed towards the canteen but Pearl had lost her appetite.

'Zinc oxide tape, like we all tape our fingers with,' she said. 'All of us except Jada-Rae, that is,' she added, looking at the calluses on her palms. 'She never uses tape.'

'And who was there just before Isla's bar routine?' said Ryan, pausing at the foot of the stairs.

'All the squad, Miss Cazacu, Coach Squibb, Dr Pond,' said Pearl.

‘We can’t tell a soul about this,’ breathed Ryan. ‘Anyone could be responsible.’

Sat 26 Jul

Ryan
Aashni really didn't like Isla, did she?
21:20

Pearl
She's just a tough crowd.
21:21

Ryan
Hamish hates how mean Isla is to him.
21:25

Pearl
Siblings fight. It's not a crime. Anyway, thought you were mates?
21:25

Ryan
Coach Squibb called Isla 'the Whinger'. Pretty mean. Could it be him?
21:29

Pearl

He calls everyone names. Night. Lights out now.

21:30

Ryan

Only Dr Pond has access to scalpels. And she's got endless zinc oxide tape.

21:40

Pearl

True.

21:41

Ryan

We should keep an eye on her.

21:42

Pearl

OK. Let's start tonight.

21:43

29

THE GREYING BEARD

By the time Jada-Rae had begun her nightly snoring, Pearl was already late for Ryan. She slipped on a hoodie and tracksuit bottoms and sneaked out. The corridor was striped with diagonals of moonlight. Pearl picked her way along, placing each foot carefully. Her heart pounded, as if it too knew the consequences of getting caught. The stairwell was eerily quiet. To her right, the canteen was dark and empty. To her left, Rest and Recovery was at rest. The back exit was already ajar, propped open with a stone. She squeezed through.

In the car park, the air smelt of grass, pine and petrol. A breeze made Pearl shiver as she crept out past the darkened cars. In socks, she stepped carefully over to the path by the Staff Only maisonettes. She joined a silhouette crouching behind a wheelie bin.

'Dr Pond's got a shopping problem,' whispered Ryan.

'Huh?' Pearl popped her head above the bin. Through the window, Dr Pond was unwrapping a series of shoe-box-shaped packages. She unboxed a pair of fancy trainers, tossing the bubblewrap aside.

'Wow, she really likes spending,' said Pearl, watching her unbox an identical pair of trainers in a lighter shade. 'But why would that make her want to injure the gymnasts?'

Ryan just put his finger to his lips. In the distance came the sound of an engine. Round the corner of Leaping Spires, a car crawled, headlights dipped. The lights swept across the lawns and down the Staff Only row of maisonettes. Pearl and Ryan pressed themselves flat against the bins, hoping they hadn't been spotted. Tyres crunched over gravel. The engine switched off. The path went dark again. It was quiet except for the ticking of the engine. They peered around.

The car was still. Moonlight bounced off the front window, revealing a *Eurohire* sticker and the shadows of two people in the front seats. Pearl froze as the passenger side door opened. The internal light clicked on. A middle-aged man with a greying beard sat in the driver's seat, while a woman climbed out from the passenger side.

'He looks so familiar,' whispered Ryan. 'Like I've seen him in an old gymnastics annual or something.'

As the woman straightened up, Pearl inhaled sharply. She absolutely recognized her. They both did. It was Miss Cazacu. Her tracksuit was gone, and instead she wore a floral dress. She had a pair of high heels in one hand, and with the other she was stuffing her golden notebook into an embroidered clutch bag. She looked girlish and sweet, not like a woman who spent all day stretching gymnasts' legs over their heads until they cried.

'She can't see us,' whispered Pearl. 'We'll get expelled.'

The car reversed out of the car park and disappeared round the edge of Leaping Spires. Its shadow slipped behind the glass. Pearl remembered to breathe again. Until the bird-like silhouette of Miss Cazacu began tip-toeing down the path. She was heading directly towards them.

'Her apartment's behind us,' gasped Ryan.

Pearl glanced behind her, feeling suddenly chilly. Past the end of the Staff Only maisonettes lay the shadowed lawns. Beyond it swished the one place they might not be seen. She tugged Ryan's arm before sprinting across the grass, hoping the dark would conceal them. As they felt the night breeze in their hair, questions swirled around Pearl's mind. It felt like every adult in the camp had a secret. And not one of them she understood.

30

THE SNATCHED PHONE

The fronds of the weeping willow fell like a curtain, keeping out prying eyes. Midges buzzed.

'Maybe Isla isn't the only victim,' said Ryan. He paced up and down by the trunk, stress radiating out of him. 'Could someone be targeting all the top gymnasts? There was Zoe's fall before you arrived. I heard she complained her rope was greasy. And Mo's slip. Remember Isla's itchy hands and Ella's leotards too? Can't all be bad luck. Must be a pattern.'

Pearl shivered. The shadows felt darker. The air felt colder. Suddenly making the team felt like a dangerous pursuit. Now she was in position to get selected, would the saboteur come after her? Or Ryan? She decided something:

'We need to find out who's doing this before they get to us.'

Ryan decided something too:

'I'm calling my mum. She'll know what to do.' He took his phone out of his pocket. The screen lit up as he swiped it. Pearl lunged for it.

'No!' She grabbed it off him, holding it over her head. 'Gloria will just pull us out of camp.'

Ryan jumped up for the phone. Pearl leapt backwards, over to the trunk. In two swift movements she was up on the lower branch.

'Maybe she'd be right to,' said Ryan from below. 'Come on, whoever's injuring the gymnasts might come after you or me next. Do you want that?'

'Do you want to give up both of our chances for the Cup?' said Pearl, tiptoeing backwards. The branch swayed over the inky lake. 'We can both qualify from here. This is everything we ever wanted.' Her voice cracked. 'It's everything Mum dreamt of for both of us.'

Ryan sighed. His glasses caught the moonlight.

'You think Coach Renshu would have wanted us to risk getting hurt?'

Silence spread along the branch. This was as close as

they got to talking about Mum.

'I never got to ask,' croaked Pearl, voice small. She turned and balanced her way out over the water.

'Don't, Pearl. You'll drop my phone,' sighed Ryan.

Pearl put a hand down and dropped into a straddle. The branch bounced gently. Still gripping the phone, she arched back and up into a handstand.

'Just come down, you don't know how deep the water is.' His voice went higher and tighter.

Pearl rotated around and lowered herself to standing.

'Why are you so scared of everything now?' she said, irritated. There was a time Ryan would have dive-bombed straight into the lake. Not any more.

She stepped back along the branch. Ryan shifted along beneath her, spotting her every step. Pearl reached the trunk.

'Promise I won't call,' said Ryan, holding up his hand for his phone.

Pearl hesitated, halfway down the trunk: 'We need to find out how many of the other accidents were suspicious. If there's anything that connects them. A pattern.'

'How are we going to do that?'

Pearl drank in the night. The breeze rustled the weeping willow.

'I know a way, but you won't like it.'

Ryan groaned.

'OK.' He grabbed her hand, drawing her and his phone in safely. However, as they walked silently back to Leaping Spires, it felt like no part of it was safe any more.

31

THE DIP IN THE GRASS

It was six-fifteen a.m. on a grey Monday morning. The sun was hidden under heavy clouds. The grass was still thick with dew. The birds were only just stirring. However, all the Mini Elites were outside, doing their five-kilometre run. They jogged around the perimeter of the lawns in sleepy obedience.

The gymnasts stretched out in single file, speeding up as they completed the loop and headed to the canteen. Pearl and Ryan jogged side by side. It was quiet, save for the shuffle of footsteps and monosyllabic grunts.

'Hey!' said Jada-Rae cheerily, slowing down to join them.

'Hey,' smiled Pearl. Ryan nodded coldly. The three of them jogged in silence for a moment, before Jada-Rae overtook them.

'Come on, slow coaches, breakfast is calling!' she called over her shoulder. But neither of them sped up.

Pearl checked behind her. They were at the back, except for Hamish. He lagged fifty paces behind, taking a laid-back approach to cardio training.

'Now,' whispered Ryan.

Pearl exhaled slowly. She looked down at a slight wrinkle in the otherwise entirely horizontal lawn. Every muscle in her body shouted, '*Nooooo!*' as she let her body flop like a sack of potatoes. A smack of impact as she landed on the grass. She clutched her ankle. She yelped in mock-agony. Ryan knelt down beside her.

'You OK?' called Jada-Rae, rushing back. Her face was full of worry.

'My ankle,' moaned Pearl, her neck prickling guiltily at the lie. 'Tripped on that stupid dip in the grass.' She gestured behind her.

'Oh, no.' Jada Rae leant in, gently trying to prise Pearl's hand off her ankle. 'Let me see.' Her breath was warm and sweet. Pearl stayed crunched up in a ball.

'I've got this,' said Ryan, helping Pearl up. 'I'll take you to the medical room.' He crowded Jada-Rae out of the way.

It was a bit rude, but Pearl appreciated it, because she wasn't sure how long she could lie to Jada-Rae.

'You sure?' said Jada-Rae to Pearl, ignoring Ryan. 'I've got ice packs in our room.'

Hamish caught up with them, his shock of red hair bouncing to a stop.

'Can I help?' he said, offering a hand.

'No, you both keep running,' said Pearl, leaning against Ryan. 'It's not too bad.'

Jada-Rae stood up, frowning.

'Hope it's OK for Saturday's assessment.' She started jogging backwards and away. 'Keep performing like you have been, we could be podium buddies in Paris!' She gave a double thumbs up and jogged off with Hamish. Pearl grinned, but seeing Ryan's pinched face, her smile died.

'We might not get to Paris if we don't stop the saboteur,' he muttered as they made their way in, Pearl leaning on his shoulder. Paris suddenly seemed a long way away.

32

THE FAKE INJURY

Pearl sat on the trolley bed in the medical room, foot out. Dr Pond examined her ankle with precise movements.

'Does it hurt here?' she said, pressing the soft flesh under her ankle bone. Pearl winced, curling her face up in pretend pain. She glanced over at the surgical instruments neatly placed in a tray on the bedside countertop: curved scissors, gauzes, forceps, clamps, zinc oxide tape and scalpels. Her gaze rested on the spare scalpel blades before moving to the lever arch files on the shelf above the desk.

'How about here?' said Dr Pond. She bent her foot

forward. Pearl nodded furiously, looking Dr Pond dead in the eye.

'And this?' suggested Dr Pond, bending her foot back the other way. Pearl nodded and pulled a pained face.

'Old injuries can play up, but this is positive, there's no swelling yet.' Her walkie-talkie crackled into life.

'Go ahead,' responded Dr Pond calmly.

'Dr Pond to the pommels gymnasium,' said a young, boyish voice.

'Who's speaking?'

'Dr Pond to the pommels gymnasium immediately,' repeated the voice.

'Back shortly,' said Dr Pond, picking up her first-aid kit. As the door closed after her, Pearl leapt off the bed. In two strides she was across the room. She sprang on to the office chair, steadying it as it spun, then on to the desk. She reached up to the shelf of lever arch files. She eased the last file off the shelf, marked: *Injuries – July*. If she could find a pattern to the injuries, maybe it could lead them to the saboteur.

Feeling sick with nerves, she flicked through the file. The pages held short descriptions of injuries, alongside the patient's name and a price. They were bills, all payable to Dr Pond:

Initial assessment of severe back injury – Isla McMorrow £300

Ongoing treatment for hand rash – Isla McMorrow £500

She turned to another page.

Concussion observation – Mo Varma £250

Knee treatment – Mo Varma £1,400

And again.

Emergency treatment of back and wrist injury – Zoe Smith £500

The door swung open. Ryan's spiky hair popped through.

'She's coming back,' he said, going pale. Pearl clicked open the arch rings and pulled out the last few pages, stuffing them into her tracksuit.

'Hurry!'

Pearl's hands shook as she replaced the file on the shelf. She jumped down, sweating with stress. Dr Pond walked in to see Pearl standing by the desk, tracksuit zipped up to her throat.

'Ankle better already?' said Dr Pond, narrowing her eyes.

Pearl looked down. All her weight was on her 'bad' ankle.

'Much better, thanks,' she blushed. Dr Pond put down her first-aid kit and moved closer.

'What's this really about, Pearl?'

Pearl stuttered, feeling the invoices shifting under her tracksuit.

'Are you coping OK? Missing home? Is it the pressure?' She looked at her sadly with earnest, grey eyes. 'As an Elite, there's so much invested by coaches, parents, everyone – it's easy to think you have no right to want anything, other than gold medals. But you should question what you lose in order to win. There are some things you should never give up on – like friends, family or your soul.'

Pearl bit her lip, feeling guilty at her deception. However, needs must. Dr Pond sighed.

'Off you go.'

Pearl hurried out to join Ryan, Dr Pond's grave words buzzing in her ears.

Round the corner, she fished the pages out of her track-suit. As Ryan read through them, his eyes widened under his glasses.

'Do you see a pattern with the injuries?' said Pearl, biting her nails.

'Not exactly, but look how much money she's getting paid,' said Ryan. 'I don't get it. Is she getting a cash bonus for every injury?'

'Well, if she is, maybe that's fair enough. More injuries mean more work for her,' suggested Pearl.

'But that's motive for causing injuries,' Ryan breathed. 'And she does have a spending problem.'

Pearl felt sick. Dr Pond couldn't be responsible, could she? A medic causing the injuries she treated? She thought of the doctor's fondness for buying expensive trainers. Were the injury bonuses how she afforded it? Then she remembered the sad look in Dr Pond's eyes and struggled to believe the worst of her.

'But I was with her when Mo slipped on the Fruitogade,' she said, thinking back to her fainting incident. Though, of course, Dr Pond had given her orange Fruitogade as she recovered. This seemed a strange coincidence.

'Well, if it's not her, who is it?' Ryan asked. Pearl had no answer. A bell rang, filling the corridor with gymnasts and reminders of the third Cup assessment. Suddenly Leaping Spires felt an altogether more dangerous place to do gymnastics.

33

A SPOONFUL OF SUGAR

Across the matting in the vaulting gym, motivational quotes were stencilled in gold. Pearl read them once more, blinking them into focus:

WINNING ISN'T EVERYTHING, IT'S THE ONLY THING.

PAIN IS YOUR FRIEND.

WINNER TAKES GOLD.

She clenched and unclenched her fists. A week of obsessing about who was causing the injuries had neither helped her training, nor got her closer to the truth. Now she needed to concentrate on what really mattered that afternoon: acing it in her vault performance.

'Happy Saturday everyone. Today is the third Cup assessment of four, so I want to see your best performances,' trilled Miss Cazacu to the assembled boys and girls. 'Nothing average, please.' Now she was back in her shiny tracksuit and trainers, it seemed impossible they had ever seen her in a dress, let alone with heels.

'Competition conditions. No mistakes. No stoppages. We must all forget about last week's drama and focus on our gymnastics.' Whispers rippled along the line of gymnasts. Isla was getting surgery on a broken shoulder that would take a season to heal. Pearl nodded to herself. Focusing on her gymnastics had never felt so difficult, what with the Cup selection at stake and a saboteur on the loose. However, focus she must. Against all odds, she was in line to make the team, with everything to win and everything to lose.

As the boys' assessment began, Dr Pond edged in through a side door. She sat quietly on a bench at the back. Pearl stiffened. Of course it was natural for the medic to be there, but still. Pearl watched her hawk-like, monitoring her every move: Dr Pond checked Hamish's shoulders, chatted to Mrs Lulu, taped Aashni's ankle. Pearl glanced across to see Ryan sticking his landing neatly, as sure and simple as ever. Then back to Dr Pond.

'Hey, you're up,' smiled Jada-Rae, sitting down beside her.

Pearl shook herself out and made her way over to the vault run-up. Each gymnast had two attempts, with the score an average of both. She cracked her neck to the side, feeling eyes on her. Not just Miss Cazacu's, peering from behind her notebook, but all the girls'. They were all watching, waiting. Knowing she'd performed well last week. Knowing her performance affected their chance of success.

She looked at the vault from the end of the run-up. A salute to Miss Cazacu with a gritted teeth smile. She started her sprint. Her feet pounded the track. As she drew closer to the springboard, she saw the slightest glinting on it – shards of something reflective. She balked, pulling up short, just in front of it. What was that? She leant forward, inspecting. The centre of the springboard was covered in a fine smear of sharp granules. Demerara brown sugar, maybe? The crunchy, rocky kind. Just enough to slide on. Or was she being paranoid? She reached forward to touch it. Had it been there before? She didn't think so.

'Stop!' Miss Cazacu's voice rose an octave. Pearl froze. 'Competition conditions, I said. Touch the springboard, I must disqualify you.'

'But it's . . .' Pearl straightened up. Miss Cazacu's look was cold.

'Champions don't fuss. One point deduction. You have

thirty seconds to restart.'

The seconds ticked down. Pearl hurried back to the start, tightening her ponytail nervously. Was someone trying to put her off her stride?

'Ten seconds.'

She hesitated. Her dreams were disintegrating before her eyes. All the glitter turning to mud. *Come on! For Mum!*

'Five.'

Pearl began. Twenty-five metres of run-up. But she knew the sugar was ahead. How could she focus on getting to maximum speed, knowing that was waiting for her? How could she be sure of getting her steps right? The sugar winked at her as she approached the springboard. She found herself shortening her steps, like a pony refusing to showjump, and then landing her feet at the front of the springboard, where the bounce was weaker, but sugar-free. It wasn't enough. Not enough speed. Not enough bounce. Not enough power. She was penguin-sliding across the vault table. The pearls pinged off her leotard as she sailed over the table, coming to an inelegant stop. She flopped over the end, bum in the air. There was a collective gasp. Pearl's ears burnt in shame.

She walked back to the springboard, gave it a brush down. A few last granules scattered off. Hardly enough to count as evidence. She looked at Miss Cazacu. Should she complain? Seeing her hard stare, Pearl thought better of it.

She dusted down the back of her feet and made her way to the start, her legs feeling like lead weights. Even as she did her second vault, sticking her landing in style, she knew there was no chance of recovering from her mess-up on the first. She stumbled out of the gym, catching Miss Cazacu's disappointed gaze. She didn't need to watch the other routines to know she would now be in last position. She might have performed well on floor and excellently on bars, but with a vault performance like that, any chance of selection now rested on her weakest event – beam. Even with all the Positive Mental Attitude in the world, it edged on impossible.

As she rushed to the locker rooms, Ryan stopped her.

'Hey, wait up,' called a voice like honey. Jada-Rae was coming too. Ryan groaned.

'What happened?' they both said together.

'There was something on the springboard.'

'Are you sure?' said Jada-Rae, wrinkling her nose, unimpressed. 'It was fine for everyone else.'

Pearl hesitated.

'I believe you,' snapped Ryan.

Pearl's two friends stared at each other. Their mutual dislike was obvious.

'So vault was a mess-up,' said Jada-Rae softly, turning back to Pearl. 'But you can recover your scores on the last assessment. It's not impossible. I'll help you. Let's just focus one hundred per cent on that. Like Miss Cazacu says, excuses are just a distraction.'

Head bowed, Pearl listened to Jada-Rae's plan for all the extra training they could do. When she looked up, she realized, with a twinge of guilt, that Ryan had gone.

34

THE FOLDED NOTE

Pearl slept badly. She dreamt she was on the lawns of Leaping Spires. A storm was raging, twisting the sodden trees. She was cartwheeling furiously forward. Among the grass were snakes and traps. The snakes slithered, ready to bite; the traps glinted, ready to snap. However, she could not stop. Because standing in the centre of the lake was the slight silhouette of a woman with shiny, black hair and dimpled cheeks. It was Mum, pirouetting endlessly. She spun away over the water, and Pearl tumbled faster to reach her. A trap snapped on her fingers, cutting into them, jolting her awake.

She sat up, half-hearing faint footsteps. It was just

before dawn, and the room was swathed in dark grey. On the floor in front of the door was a folded note. It seemed to glow in the dark. Who was it from? Careful not to wake Jada-Rae, Pearl clambered down the bunk ladder. Her heart was still thumping; her fingers were still trembling. However, when she bent to pick up the note, it was gone.

Pearl straightened up, confused at where dream ended and waking began. She realized the note had had an impossible dreamy glow to its edges anyway. She leant against the door, listening to the rhythmic rising and falling of Jada-Rae's breath.

Remembering the footsteps, she carefully opened the door and slipped out. Silence stretched down the sleeping corridor. Pearl crept along, listening. The stairwell spun down. She stood on the first-floor landing for a moment, blinking the sleep from her eyes. Was that a noise? She tiptoed down the stairs. The double doors to the gymnasiums seemed to quiver. She rubbed her eyes. Then slipped through.

The Hall of Fame was as still as a graveyard. She hurried along, then stopped. If someone had been there, they were long gone. She was left with the frozen smiles of the framed gymnasts. And one particular gymnast who had been smiling at her from a faded frame since she arrived.

Finally, she looked. The photo was of four girls in

matching GB tracksuits. They leant into each other, arms draped over shoulders with the casualness of good friends. A true team. In the centre stood a young girl with shiny, black hair and dimples just like her own. *Renshu Chui – Team GB*. This was Mum at her happiest.

Pearl stood drinking it in. As she did, a memory popped into her head. The last call with Mum.

It all happened so fast. When Dad hung up it said *2 mins 02* on the screen. Just over two minutes to say all their goodbyes, before Mum's breathing broke into laboured snatches and the doctor took over.

Max didn't even make it down the stairs in time. Pearl never knew what Mum said to Dad because he walked into the hallway, swallowing each stilted word.

'I will . . . I will . . . So are you, Renshu . . . Let me pass you over.' As he came back in with the phone, he turned away so Pearl didn't see his face. He stood behind her, a hand on each shoulder. On the screen, Pearl saw Mum's dry lips, oxygen mask marks denting her drawn cheeks, eyes sallow. Her mum, but with all her smiles removed.

It had been the day before Pearl's eleventh birthday. She was convinced Mum was calling to say she'd taken a turn for the better and would be home by tomorrow. Pearl had started rabbiting on about how they could make a cake together – to celebrate both of their special days.

'Pearl,' croaked Mum. 'Pearl.' Pearl continued, hurrying into telling Mum about the new vault skill she wanted to show her. Mum interrupted again.

'I need you to listen.' She broke into a wheeze.

Pearl sat down at the kitchen table, finally taking in the unwelcome rasp.

'They're going to intubate me. You know what that might mean, don't you?'

Pearl could only answer with the tiniest 'mmm'.

'Now be strong for Dad and Max, won't you?'

Again, all she could reply was a tiny, high-pitched 'mmm'.

'You light up the world with your shine, OK.'

Pearl nodded hard, squeaking back an 'OK'.

Now as Pearl stood, eyeing the framed photo, she knew there was no way she was giving up. Not a chance in the world. For Mum, she would sacrifice anything to make the team. She would cartwheel through snakes, traps and anyone in her way. Whatever the risk, whatever the danger, sabotage or no, she was going to succeed. Come what may.

35

THE BLOODIED NOSE

Pearl woke before Jada-Rae. She brushed her teeth, slipped on her leotard, brushed her hair into a bun and white-spirited her calluses. The sweet, chemical smell filled the room, making Pearl cough. Still Jada-Rae snored. She shook her awake. Jada-Rae groaned and rolled over.

'I'm going to need an unbelievable score on beam. Will you help me?'

Jada-Rae sat up, rubbing her eyes.

'Let's do it,' she replied with a sleepy laugh.

Ten minutes later they had sneaked down to the beams and pommels gym, and Pearl was demonstrating her routine. She finished safely with a backwards tuck dismount. Knees bent, she raised her arms. Jada-Rae counted in her head, scribbled in her tiny, white notebook and looked at Pearl.

'Well?' said Pearl, coming over. She sat down in butterfly position, knees out, feet pulled in close.

'I mean, you're really neat, but your difficulty levels are too low, like your buddy Ryan's. You know that, right? Skip leaps won't get you selected.'

Pearl nodded. She wasn't going to be keeping it simple like Ryan any more. She unfastened her hand grips and rubbed her wrists. They had a dull ache in them that she'd never noticed before. Maybe that's what seven days a week of training did.

'Hey, you ever tried the Cazacu?' said Jada-Rae, putting down her notebook.

Pearl shook her head nervously. The Cazacu dismount was notoriously difficult. A backwards layout with double twist – a double full. The move Miss Cazacu had invented in her days as an Olympic gymnast. She'd seen Jada-Rae do it, but no one else. Pearl thought about Ryan's podcast tagline: *train safe and train smart*. Doing the Cazacu was neither safe nor smart. It might help her win, though, in spite of what Ryan would think.

'It would really increase your difficulty scores. Would

definitely put you in the running. Think you could do it. Watch.'

Jada-Rae leapt up on to the beam. Then, without hesitation, she threw herself into a huge round off. She catapulted the length of the beam, building speed. Up and off the end, flipping into a backwards layout. As she flipped over herself like a needle on a compass, she also corkscrewed round, not once, but twice. She landed, her face full of concentration. Then turned to Pearl with a relieved grin.

'Always a bit scary. But worth it.' She sat down, legs pointed out in front of her. She cracked a bone in her neck. As if she'd just demonstrated something as simple as boiling an egg.

Pearl wasn't sure. She could do one twist, she knew. But two? What if she didn't make it? She thought of Gloria. She wouldn't approve. She'd say it was too hard. That she'd need to learn it in stages. First on a harness. Then into a foam pit. Not in just one secret Sunday morning session.

'You can do it!' nodded Jada-Rae.

There was nothing for it. Not with the power of Jada-Rae's confidence in her. The trust of a true friend. If she could nail this, she could make the team. So, propelled by friendship, she got to her feet and mounted the beam.

Dawn rays warming her cheeks, she walked through

the move in her head, making tiny practice motions with her hands. Round off to the end. Backwards layout. Twist. Twist. Land. She rubbed the fear out of her face and cricked her neck. The matting below suddenly looked very hard. But there was nothing for it. She swallowed. She was off.

Adrenaline pumping, she took a single running step and then threw herself forward. Her hands pressed against the beam as she sprang upside down. Then powered upwards. Twisting and flipping to land upright. Before pushing off the end of the beam. She was airborne. Body poker straight. She stretched out as she flipped back, praying she'd gained enough height. As she reached fully upside down she rotated her body sideways. Once. The matting careered towards her. Almost twice. The landing happened. Too hard. Too fast. Her body crunched together with the impact. Her face whiplashed into her knees. Pain cracked her cheekbone. Pressure drove through her legs, forcing a step forward on to her weaker ankle. With her nose bloodied by her own knees, and her twinging ankle a reminder of her old injury, she straightened.

A whoop from the side. Jada-Rae was on her feet, clapping.

'Almost, you can do it!' she yelled, before remembering they weren't supposed to be there. She quietened down.

Later, Pearl lay on Jada-Rae's bed with one ice pack on her nose and another on her ankle. She looked at the poster of the young Elena Cazacu, thinking. A little further on the second twist, without that step, and she'd stick the Cazacu. She could make the team. Have a real chance of winning gold. She thought of Mum and how her cheeks would have dimpled to see Pearl on the podium. A smile broke across her bruising, bloodied face.

Sun 3 Aug

Ryan

I just saw Hamish coming out of Dr Pond's room. He looked pretty shifty.

07:31

Ryan

Is Dr Pond still in the canteen?

07:32

Ryan

You don't think he could have stolen the scalpel?

07:33

Ryan

He did complain every night about Isla.

07:34

Ryan

When Mo slipped, he was the first one there. He's gone up in the rankings now.

07:35

Ryan

I'm going to keep an eye on him.

07:36

Ryan

Hello?

07:37

Pearl

Sorry, skipped breakfast for extra training with Jada-Rae. She's helping me learn the Cazacu. Think I can get it in time for the last assessment.

11:00

Ryan

Thought you wanted to find out who's causing the injuries. Not cause yourself one.

11:03

36

THE SLIPPED SCARF

The last week at Leaping Spires brought a heatwave and the cranking up of the air conditioning. It also brought a hot wave of rivalry. Ranking scores were analysed. Difficulty levels of routines were counted. Every bend and twist was assessed. Friendliness in the squad dried up, as the gymnasts chased even the slightest chance to impress. All because Saturday was days away – the final assessment, after which Miss Cazacu would be announcing the Cup team.

She stood on a beam in the beams and pommels gym, addressing the gymnasts as they jogged past her.

'In the Cup, there can be no sloppy foot placings. You

must know your apparatus blindfolded. Be able to do your routines in your sleep. So today, you will be doing a special challenge. You will walk through your beam routine . . . without the aid of sight. Big tumbles and your dismount you may skip. All other elements you must perform.' A collective gasp from the gymnasts, as they switched to jogging backwards. Pearl caught a rare look of concern on Jada-Rae's face.

Coach Squibb held up a clear box full of silk scarves.

'One each,' he grimaced. 'Line up.'

The gymnasts lined up obediently in front of him. It felt too dangerous, but who would be brave enough to say no? Especially with Miss Cazacu looking on. In turn they picked out a scarf and each took their seats by their equipment.

Pearl queued behind Jada-Rae, feeling sick.

'Choose the thinnest, lightest one you can,' she whispered over her shoulder. Pearl nodded without hesitation.

Coach Squibb held out the box of scarves while Pearl rummaged through. She picked up a thin, white scarf. She could just about see her fingers through it.

'Not that one,' he snapped, nostrils flaring. Pearl retracted her hand like she'd touched a hot coal. 'Hurry up.'

Pearl grabbed the nearest scarf. It was thick and red like congealed blood. This did not bode well. She sat down beside Jada-Rae near the beams.

They watched the routines, counting down to their own. The gymnasts went one by one, every face grim with concentration. Leaps were lower. Flips were fewer. Falls were frequent. Only Aashni was as sure-footed as always. However, even she toned down her routine. Finishing, she pulled off her scarf to reveal a scowl that could singe granite.

'More like a safety drill, that,' sneered Coach Squibb into Miss Cazacu's ear. Only at Ella's turn did his remarks dwindle away. Her routine was as neat as her coiled plaits. She struck pose after pose, dip-walking nimbly between them. Every leap was high; every landing was stuck cleanly. Back arched, she twisted around with a winsome smile.

'That's not fair,' said Pearl, nudging Jada-Rae. She pointed at Ella's scarf. It was the same thin, white scarf Coach Squibb had refused to let her use.

Jada-Rae shrugged, fixing her own scarf. 'With Coach Squibb's favourite, it's never going to be fair.' She fiddled with the knot, sliding the scarf higher up her forehead. 'That's why you've got to find a way to even things out. Wish me luck,' she said, standing up. She tipped her head back so Pearl could see the whites of her eyes through a gap under the scarf. She winked.

Pearl watched guiltily as Jada-Rae performed her routine at full difficulty. Aerial cartwheels followed back handsprings followed side saltos. It was impressive. Even Coach Squibb couldn't deny that. Miss Cazacu scribbled approvingly in her golden notebook.

Pearl was up. She tiptoed over to the beam, fingering her scarf thoughtfully. Jada-Rae jumped down. Taking the scarf out of Pearl's hand, she wrapped it over Pearl's eyes.

'Hey, let me tip it back, just a little,' she whispered, adjusting the knot. 'I'll tighten it over your forehead, not your eyes.' Was it cheating? Especially if everyone else was doing it?

'But . . .' Pearl could see about half a metre's diameter below her, like a blinkered horse. She couldn't quite bring herself to refuse.

She mounted the beam, feeling Miss Cazacu's eyes on her. Her body went into autopilot as she twisted, turned and tiptoed along. Her crouching pirouette was so honed with practice she just felt her way through it. And her muscle memory lifted her into an arabesque. However, as she reached her leap series, she took guilty glance after guilty glance down. Through the gap in her scarf, she checked her position on every skip leap and tuck jump. As she prepared for her final elements, she sneaked in a distance check. Thankful for that slight sliver of sight, she adjusted half a step back. With the confidence of a trickster, she flipped the length of the beam. What a finish!

As she took off her scarf to climb down, Miss Cazacu walked purposefully over. Pearl broke into an uncomfortable sweat. Had she noticed her slipped scarf?

'That was as spectacular as your vault was sub-standard. If you perform like that blindfolded, I have hope you will redeem yourself on Saturday. Do not disappoint me.'

Pearl nodded, blushing. Although it was wrong, her bending of the rules felt somehow worth it.

37

THE RIPPED MATTRESS

It was Friday night. The night before the last assessment, which meant finishing training a whole two hours early. For a treat, they were all getting to watch a movie and eat popcorn. *Summer of Somersaults* 2, Pearl's second favourite movie of all time. Only surpassed by the original *Summer of Somersaults*. Jada-Rae had saved Pearl a front row seat. However, Pearl wasn't there, because Ryan had found evidence of sabotage. Lots of it.

They slipped down the boys' corridor. Pearl hadn't been there before. It smelt of damp towels and sweaty gym shorts. Ryan walked ahead, twitching with twiddle-toed tension.

'You're sure there's no other explanation,' whispered Pearl, tight on his shoulder. Ryan shook his head stubbornly, turning into his and Hamish's room.

On the top bunk, Ryan beckoned Pearl. She didn't need to ask whose bunk was whose. Ryan would be on the bottom, on account of the danger of falling out of bed in his sleep. Pearl scrambled up. Their heads came together as Ryan twisted over the edge of the mattress. There was a rip along the side, just by the seam.

'I heard him rustling about with it in the night. Put your hand in.'

Pearl stuck her hand in. She felt something cold and hard. She pulled out a scalpel. Her heart fluttered uneasily.

'There's more,' muttered Ryan. He looked like he might faint with the stress of it all.

Pearl leant in again. She pulled out a screwdriver, then a small bottle of lubricant. Pearl held it in the palm of her hand. She read the label:

Hi-Performance R/C Model Grease – Contains PTFE

'Perfect for greasing a rope, right?' breathed Ryan. 'You know Zoe fell off one of the high ropes.' He pushed his off-duty glasses up his nose, his eyes wide.

She pulled out a pair of wire cutters. They were small enough to slip into a tracksuit pocket but still powerful.

'You could fray a bars wire with those,' nodded Ryan.

Pearl pulled out the final objects: a pair of tiny pliers and a small spanner.

'Saboteur kit,' whispered Ryan. 'He must be planning his next injury.'

Pearl felt sick.

They both jumped, as the door swung open.

Hamish stood in the doorway, red hair reflecting the hall light.

'Not a fan of movies?' he said casually.

He raised his hands up to the top of the door frame and used it to swing into the room. Pearl tried to subtly gather up the tools. They clanked guiltily.

'I'm no big fan of *Summer of Somersaults* 2 myself.' He placed his hands on the end of the bunk bed and hurdled up. He landed in a crouch in front of Pearl and Ryan. The tools lay between them.

Ryan flattened himself against the back wall.

'But I'm also no fan of people sneaking into my room and going through my stuff.' He threw a pillow at Ryan's head.

Batting it away, Ryan held up the can of oil: 'Yeah, well, what's this for?'

'None of your business,' said Hamish, folding his arms.

'And this?' said Ryan, holding up the scalpel. 'We know

how you injured Isla.'

Now Hamish looked stunned.

'What? You think I'd injure my sister?' he snorted. His cheeks went as red as his hair.

He turned to Pearl. 'My own twin?' His hostility hummed around the room. 'You want to know my secret? Check my other hiding place.'

Pearl looked at Ryan. All his certainty had ebbed away, his eyebrows becoming question marks.

'Oh. You haven't found it yet? It's just here.' He leant back and dipped his hand into the side of the mattress at the end. He pulled out a small cardboard box. He placed it in front of them.

'Maybe I just keep some things private, so my sister doesn't tease me. Like how I bet you'd like to keep it private that you call your mum and cry about missing your old coach every night,' he said, glaring at Ryan.

Now it was Ryan's turn to go red.

'Yeah. I heard you,' continued Hamish. 'But I never said anything – everyone gets homesick. I can't believe I tried to look out for you. Pah.'

He swung down from the bunk bed and walked out. He didn't even bother to slam the door. Pearl decided never to bring up what Hamish had said.

They both looked at each other, then lunged for the

box. It creaked open. Inside was a tiny, remote-controlled car, no bigger than a hand's width, and a small controller.

'Oh,' said Ryan in a small voice.

Pearl picked up the car. Tiny wheels, oiled to perfection. Shiny screws. A neat engine like a beating heart.

'Could still be a cover story,' said Ryan.

Pearl rolled her eyes.

'Or maybe you just made an enemy of your really friendly room-mate? How about you stop jumping to conclusions about totally innocent people?' With that, Pearl left Ryan to it. She had popcorn to eat and screentime to enjoy with Jada-Rae. Tonight, she wanted a break from Ryan and his ill-judged accusations.

Sat 9 Aug

Ryan

If Hamish didn't do it, who did?

05:59

Pearl

Good morning to you too.

06:02

Ryan

This is serious.

06:02

Pearl

Our assessment is serious. It's in 3 hours.

06:02

Ryan

Can we talk? Meet you in the equipment cupboard in ten.

06:02

Pearl

Jada-Rae and I are just walking through our routines. And it's breakfast in ten.

06:04

Ryan

Please? I wouldn't ask if it wasn't important.

06:04

Pearl

Fine.

06:05

38

THE CHALK CIRCLE

Pearl sat cross-legged in the cramped equipment cupboard, on a pile of mats so high they almost reached the ceiling. A good place for a private discussion, apparently. Ryan sat beside her, arms wrapped round his knees.

'So what was so important you needed me to skip breakfast?' she asked, belly rumbling. 'Hardly the best preparation for our last assessment.'

'Pearl. You're not going to like what I'm going to say.' Ryan took off his off-duty glasses, rubbed them on his vest then put them back on. 'I'm not sure about Jada-Rae. You should be careful of her.'

'Seriously?' Pearl shook her head and uncrossed her legs. She swivelled, eyeballing him.

Ryan fidgeted his fingers.

'I just don't know if she's always got your back. She's always pushing you to train too much, take risks you shouldn't. Like doing the Cazacu.'

Pearl opened and shut her mouth, furious and speechless. She jumped down, landing neatly between a cluster of standing chalk bowls and a box of ropes.

'Statistically speaking, you're most likely . . .'

She cut him off.

'She's just trying to help me succeed, Ryan. You've got to push yourself to win. Just because you won't take risks any more, doesn't mean I shouldn't.'

Hungry and irritable, she wound round a stack of springboards to the door. Ryan jumped down.

'Wait. There's more.'

Pearl stopped, hand on the door handle. He said it gently, almost apologetically. 'I've been wondering if she might be our saboteur.'

'You think everyone's guilty.'

'Better than fooling yourself everyone's innocent.'

Pearl felt a sudden need to inspect the handle, feeling the edge of each callus on her palm against the cold metal. No, she didn't like this. Since camp started, Jada-Rae had become a really good friend. She was becoming as close a friend as Ryan, her actual best friend. It seemed too convenient for him to decide Jada-Rae was chief suspect now. It was almost like he was jealous.

'It's just sometimes, during training, when she thinks no one's looking, I see her jotting things down in her tiny notebook.'

Pearl spun round.

'I know what's in her notebook. She's strategic. It doesn't make her the saboteur.'

'Well, the day before Isla's fall, I saw her jotting down a lot about her,' said Ryan, carefully ducking under a row of hanging hoops.

'She writes down people's routines,' said Pearl, fidgeting her fingers. 'So she can make sure she has higher difficulty levels. It makes her a good competitor, not a criminal.'

'You're beginning to sound like her.' Ryan said it like an accusation. 'Last night, I was looking out of the window in the canteen. She thought I wasn't looking at her, but I could see her in the reflection. She was watching me. Just eating her food and staring at me, for like five minutes.'

'I'm not sure that counts as evidence.'

'OK. But it was weird.'

'Maybe it was also weird that you spent five minutes watching her watching you.'

Normally Ryan would have laughed about this. However, he had mislaid his sense of humour somewhere between the foam mats and the pommel horses. Instead, he took a handful of chalk from a standing chalk bowl. He bent down and drew a chalk circle on the parquet floor between them.

'Sometimes you've got to choose who your real friends are, Pearl.'

He straightened up, and then stepped into the circle.

'So are you in? Or are you out?'

Pearl looked at the circle.

Ryan was asking her to make an impossible choice: between him and the one friend who could help her make the Cup team. She wanted to find the saboteur too, but he was being ridiculous suspecting Jada-Rae. This was taking loyalty too far.

She turned away.

'I've got to get back,' she mumbled, stumbling out of the door. 'I'm starving.' As she made her way to the canteen, she felt their friendship slowly unwinding, like cotton on a reel.

39

THE CAZACU

The last selection event arrived, with a light smattering of extra pressure. The other staff, some of the Senior Elites and even a Fruitogade executive had come to watch the boys on pommels and girls on beams. Dr Pond had set up a massage table in the corner. Coach Squibb had donned his best shorts. Mrs Lulu had brought a pair of pom-poms to cheer with. The beams and pommels gym had never been so full.

The gymnasts sat quietly on a bench, waiting to perform. Pearl jiggled her knees anxiously. If Mum had been there, she would have put a hand on Pearl's knee, stilling her nerves. Pearl kept jiggling. The silence intensified as the boys' event began. One after another, the boys flared and spun on the pommel horse like human pendulums. Hamish stumbled on his dismount. He returned to the bench, shaking his head at his score. Pearl was only half-watching though, absent-mindedly wringing her hands together. She walked through her new routine in her head, hoping Miss Cazacu would be wowed.

'Tough on Hamish,' commented Jada-Rae, finishing some notes in her notebook. 'But good for your friend. He's got a chance now. Especially with Mo injured.' Pearl watched as Ryan saluted. His eyes moved past her, as if she didn't exist. Under his elasticated glasses, he looked resolute. As he did his sequence of elements, his shape remained firm. He was strength, discipline and a stiff chin. He finished without a flinch. His score was his best yet, qualifying him for the Cup. However, he didn't look at Pearl. He just walked past and sat on the boys' bench.

'Why's Ryan being like that?' Jada-Rae whispered beside her.

'Beats me,' shrugged Pearl, sipping her water, knowing full well why.

'Maybe he doesn't like us being besties?' said Jada-Rae, loosening her shoulders. Besties? Jada-Rae had just referred to them as besties. Pearl's chest swelled.

As if in a trance, Pearl watched the girls perform their

routines. Then she was on. Her final chance, following her mess-up on vault. She stood up.

Chalking her hands, she shook off the excess in puffs of fine white. The beam stood expectantly in front of her. She knew she could do it, yet her ears buzzed with worries.

She moved through her routine, connecting the elements fluidly, but her mind raced towards the climax: to the Cazacu and all the glory it would bring.

At the end of the beam, she took a breath. Arms up, ribcage drawn high. Into the round off. Hands clutching suede, she pushed off. She spun upright, springing off the end of the beam, throwing herself backwards while leaping up. Time slowed as she flipped. Twisting, floating, spinning, hoping. The force of her layout pushed her upright as she spun around a second time. And landed. Her feet splayed, strong and firm. *Don't take a step. Stand up.* She raised her arms triumphantly. She had stuck it.

'I did not approve your new dismount,' said Miss Cazacu, making a strike in her notebook. 'A risky strategy and a risky move.' Pearl's arms dropped. 'It was, however, faultless. This time. Thirteen point two. Congratulations.'

As Pearl returned to the girls, her head spun. Jada-Rae high-fived her. Ella low-fived her. Aashni offered her bubblegum in celebration. The four of them hugged.

'International Cup, here we come,' laughed Pearl. Mum

would have been more than proud. She would have been elated.

Her laughter died away as Ryan marched, scowling, out of the gym. Suddenly, her success felt the loneliest in the world.

40

THE PROFESSIONAL LEOTARD

Selection changed everything. Pearl was no longer the last-minute injury replacement. She wasn't just 'Mini Elite Squad good', she was 'Cup team good'. She deserved her place and more. In less than a week they would be competing in Paris, beginning their sporting career on a far bigger stage. There was much to prepare, from media training to new team tracksuits to bespoke competition leotards. Which was why she was pressing the buzzer for the last door of the row of Staff Only maisonettes, feeling guilty already.

Mrs Lulu opened the door, wearing a silk, fuchsia apron covered in pins.

'Hello, poppet! I was wondering when you'd be asking for my services. You're the last one.' She flicked her extra-long ponytail, her eyes twinkling.

'I was hoping you could alter my competition leotard,' said Pearl.

'I can do better than that,' beamed Mrs Lulu, ushering her in. 'I'll make you dazzle like a gold medal!' Inside was a feast of sequins, clothes dummies and sewing machinery. Rolls of velvet, velour and spandex were propped up against every available wall. The carpet was littered with discarded strips of fabric. It was like Mrs Lulu had transported the costume department of *Strictly Come Dancing* into her front room.

'Up you get, sweetheart,' she said, pointing to a low coffee table with a full-length mirror in front of it. Pearl hopped up, unzipping her jacket. As she took off her bottoms, her gaze wandered to a photo gallery of a gymnast with the same smile as Mrs Lulu. From toddler to infant to early teen, the girl was captured in dozens of beautiful, sparkly leotards, smiling mid-cartwheel, mid-pirouette and mid-layout. Pearl guessed this must be the daughter Mrs Lulu always talked about.

'Now,' said Mrs Lulu, approaching with a measuring tape. 'What you need is a really impactful, winning leotard. An outfit that brings out your unique personality.'

Pearl looked at herself in the mirror. The light-blue material shone back at her. She ran her hand over the 'P' of plastic pearls on the shoulder. Mum had sewn on each pearl carefully, her slender fingers working delicately as she hummed to pop ballads on the radio.

'I was thinking we could just tidy this up,' said Pearl, gesturing to what she was wearing. 'Maybe add some extra crystals?'

Mrs Lulu peered at the leotard. She walked around the coffee table.

'It's a little tight. The fabric is low quality. I can alter it, but it'll be a bodge job. It's better to make you something bespoke for the Cup. The perfect look is just as important as the perfect routine if you want to be a winner.'

Pearl looked at her reflection. Her leotard seemed suddenly childish and silly, made by an amateur. 'I suppose.'

'Let me see, where are you from again?' said Mrs Lulu, taking some measurements.

'Bagley End,' said Pearl. The thought of it made her heart creak.

Mrs Lulu looked bemused.

'It's in Wales.'

'Ooh, I could do something with that!' She held some green fabric up to Pearl. 'Welsh flag is green, so I'm thinking green! And Pearl makes me think of . . . pearls!

But premium pearls. This could be terrific.' Her blue eyes shone with inspiration. She laid down the green fabric on a table, her scissors hovering over it. 'So, is it yes to a new leo?'

Pearl looked at the pearls on her shoulder. A thread was loose. She pulled it. A single plastic pearl fell off and rolled under the sofa. She hugged her elbows to herself. She couldn't bring herself to nod.

'My mum made me it,' Pearl whispered. 'She's not around any more.'

Mrs Lulu lowered her scissors. She pointed at the photo gallery of the same smiling gymnast. 'My Allegra was such a talented tumbler,' she sighed. 'Even when she was a toddler everyone could see she had star quality. I had such dreams for her, especially when she started training at Leaping Spires. I even got a job here to make things easier. Must have made her over a hundred leotards. Our whole lives were about gymnastics. That was, until she missed out on the team. She quit after that. Never even does a handstand these days.' She smiled, raising her scissors once more. 'Sometimes we have to let the things we once loved go, even if it's hard. Make room for new things.'

Pearl nodded. Mrs Lulu was right. She was doing all this for Mum, so how could she be feeling guilty about Mum? Mrs Lulu squealed with excitement, laid out the fabric on a table and began cutting.

Ninety minutes later, Pearl stepped out of the front door, feeling the softness of her new outfit under her tracksuit. It was the leotard of a champion, and it screamed success. Mrs Lulu followed her out to the wheelie bins.

'Let's dispose of this, shall we?' she said, holding up Pearl's lucky leotard. She flipped open a bin lid. 'Say good-bye to the old you?'

Pearl knew what she had to do. 'Yes, let's get rid of it.'

Mrs Lulu dropped it in the bin just as Ryan walked past, earphones on, heading for the lake alone. He caught a flash of light-blue fabric and plastic pearls. The look he gave Pearl filled her with shame.

41

THE YOUNGEST BRIDESMAID

As the last twenty-four hours of preparations were made, the team went everywhere together. In the canteen, they sat together at a separate table. In media training, they swapped notes and jokes. It was as if the list taped to the pinboard in the central stairwell followed them everywhere.

<u>International Cup team – girls</u>

Jada-Rae Williams

Aashni Patel

Ella Hart

Pearl Bolton

The day before they departed, Pearl was invited to Ella's room for the first time – to hang out with the team while they waited for their photo shoot to start.

Aashni posed in front of the mirror, chewing gum. She was already wearing her new competition leotard – a high-cut black one-piece embellished with a silver lightning mark. She glared at herself, smoothing a wrinkle in the fabric.

'Needs more impact,' she huffed. 'Aashni means "lightning" in Hindi, not "hint of lightning". Everyone needs to remember Lightning Girl at the Cup. I'll get Mrs Lulu to add more sequins.'

'My followers will love my new leo,' sighed Ella. She held up a leotard with a huge sequined heart on it. 'Though my uncle sent me this one too. Gorgeous, huh?' She showed them another heart-encrusted one, looking pained by the choice. 'Which one shall I wear for the shoot?'

'It's a tough one,' said Jada-Rae, walking on her hands over piles of discarded leotards. 'What do you think, Pearl?'

Pearl lay on the bottom bunk in her tracksuit. She wasn't quite ready to show off her new leotard, or to admit she was letting Mum's one go. Especially after the look Ryan had given her. Like she was betraying Mum or something.

'Maybe . . . ask your fans their favourite?' said Pearl, sitting up.

'Great idea,' said Ella, squeezing out of one leotard and into another. 'Can you film a livestream, Jada-Rae?'

Jada-Rae picked up Ella's phone. She attached an extra phone lens, slotted it into a tripod and pointed it at Ella.

'Ready when you are.'

'Count me out,' Aashni said, slipping on her headphones and retiring to the top bunk.

'Hang on, my make-up doesn't work with this,' said Ella, opening her make-up bag. Jada-Rae winked at Pearl and rolled her eyes. Pearl giggled.

As Ella leant into the mirror to apply mascara, Jada-Rae started flicking through Ella's phone.

'Jada-Rae!' mouthed Pearl. Jada-Rae shrugged and scrolled through messages. Pearl peered closer, despite herself. There was nothing of any interest. Just a lot of fan mail.

'Do you think pink eyeshadow for this leotard?' asked Ella, clattering through her make-up bag.

'Totally,' gabbled Pearl, turning red. Jada-Rae was going through Ella's photos now, spinning back through the years. Pearl nudged her. This was definitely invading Ella's privacy. Jada-Rae just gave her a cheeky grin back. She giggled over a photo of a much younger and geekier

Ella, dressed as Harry Potter. She scrolled to an even younger Ella with a terrible bowl haircut. Then to her in a puffy dress, the youngest bridesmaid in a family wedding shot. Pearl put a hand to Jada-Rae's wrist, stopping her moving on. All the men looked familiar. Clearly brothers, they were all heavy-set, with bushy eyebrows and big moustaches.

'Who's that?' she mouthed, pointing at a man with his arm around Ella. Jada-Rae's eyeballs popped out.

They both knew exactly who it was. Younger, slimmer, and in a snug suit, he was unmistakeable. Coach Squibb.

'No way,' whispered Jada-Rae. 'They're related? That's her mystery uncle, isn't it?'

Pearl's mouth dropped. Her brain spun in circles. Of course. It made sense of Coach Squibb's special treatment of Ella, from the endless compliments to the choice of blindfold.

'How do I look, ready for Paris?' smiled Ella, striking a pose. 'Let's shoot!'

'Ella,' said Jada-Rae slowly. 'All those special food deliveries you get, like your green muffins, they're from your uncle, aren't they?'

'Yup,' smiled Ella, still holding her pose.

'And your new leos are from him too?'

'He's my biggest fan,' shrugged Ella.

'Then why do we never see him at competitions?' continued Jada-Rae.

Ella dropped her pose.

'Why do you ask?'

'Because of this,' said Jada-Rae, turning the phone in Ella's direction.

Ella's bottom lip wobbled. 'We had to keep it a secret,' she stammered. 'Otherwise, people would think I'm only in the squad because my uncle's the coach.'

'Explains all the favouritism,' mumbled Pearl.

'I am his favourite, of course, and I tell him not to make such a fuss, but he insists. He's got no kids himself, so he'd do anything to see me succeed. Please don't tell? Especially not Aashni, she'll hate me for it.' As Ella glanced up at the top bunk, a tear rolled down her cheek. Pearl couldn't help but feel sympathy.

'We won't tell,' she said, nudging Jada-Rae.

'Fine,' shrugged Jada-Rae, doubtfully.

However, as Ella began her livestream, Jada-Rae continued to look troubled. Pearl wondered if this explained what Coach Squibb might gain from seeing his niece's rivals injured. Or if Ella could be fully trusted either.

She looked wistfully out of the window at where lake met lawn. What was Ryan up to? Certainly not hanging out with Hamish, after their fall-out. Maybe hidden somewhere, recording a podcast alone. She wished she could talk to him about these worrying new sabotage suspects. Things were different now, though. The thought of apologizing flashed through her mind, but he shouldn't have made her choose between friends. It wasn't right. Anyway, she had a newer, more winning friend to rely on now.

42

THE CLOUDY LIQUID

Pearl had never been to a photo shoot before, especially not one with a whole crew of assistants there just to make them look good. They had taken over the whole atrium, turning one section into a temporary hair and make-up area, another into a photo studio and a third into a video village for the Fruitogade executives. Pearl brushed away her suspicions about Coach Squibb and Ella, determined to enjoy herself. This was everything she'd hoped for. Everything Mum had dreamt of.

As the girls had their make-up done, Miss Cazacu moved between them. Mrs Lulu trailed behind, carrying a cup of tea for her.

'Why all the different eyeshadows? I like gold eyeshadow for all my girls.' Miss Cazacu blinked slowly, revealing gold-powdered eyelids.

The make-up artist yawned and continued to apply sparkly blusher to Pearl's cheeks. 'I'm just doing what I'm told by your sponsors, lady,' she shrugged, nodding at the suited huddle of executives sitting behind a computer monitor by a bed of peach trees.

Miss Cazacu drifted away, tutting.

Pearl didn't mind at all. They had done her hair in a Dutch braid. Plus, she had lilac eyeshadow, a new rosiness to her cheeks and lip gloss that made her lips glisten like cherries. Jada-Rae had a cute double braid and gradient tawny brown eyes. Aashni had a French plait and shocking green eyeshadow. Ella looked especially spangly. The make-up artist had even put natural-looking make-up on the boys, so their skin glowed in perfectly even tones.

She hopped up as the photographer called them over, wearing their shiny new team tracksuits. He strategically placed them for their group shot, remembering to leave enough space to feature the giant Fruitogade logo in the background. Ryan stood at the edge of the group, face neutral, beside a now unfriendly Hamish. Pearl didn't go over to talk to him, and he seemed happy to ignore her since their argument.

She watched, irritated, as he did the boys' team shots. The photographer snapped away while they drank Fruitogade on cue. What right did he have to ignore her? He was being totally unreasonable. It was her business if she did the Cazacu. Her business if she wanted to be friends with Jada-Rae. Her business if she upgraded her leotard.

Next, it was the girls' team shot. Pearl took off her tracksuit, revealing her new leotard. It fitted like a second skin. The bright green fabric was covered in an explosion of pearls. On the right sleeve was the name of the sponsor: *Fruitogade*. On the back, embroidered in pearls, her name: PEARL. It was beautiful – inspired by Mum's creation, but better. Timidly, she took her place in the team.

'Oh, wow,' said Ella, looking startled.

Aashni nodded, which for her, counted as a compliment.

'You shall go to the ball,' joked Jada-Rae.

Only Ryan looked unimpressed.

The assistant handed out bottles of brightly coloured Fruitogade. Each had their name written on a label at the back. Pearl inspected the cap. The hygiene seal had already been broken. She popped it open anyway. Fruitogade reminded her of post-training sugary feasts in the back of Gloria's minivan. She took a sip. It tasted odd. Sweet but with a chalky aftertaste she didn't recognize. She held the orange liquid up to the film lights. It was faintly cloudy, which wasn't how she remembered it. Was it a new flavour she'd never had?

'Does this taste weird to you?' she asked the others.

'I just pretend to drink the stuff,' admitted Aashni with a shrug.

'First time I've had it,' said Ella, taking a generous slug. 'But so long since I had any sugar, tastes amazing!' She guzzled a little more. She wiped her mouth guiltily.

Jada-Rae swallowed a sip. 'Tastes fine to me.'

'All take a sip when I say so,' said the photographer to the group. 'Smile! And sip!'

Pearl flashed her sunniest smile and pretend-sipped, imagining Max looking at her on a poster. He'd be pretty impressed. His sister next to all the gymnastics stars.

'Now, everyone lifting the smallest of you,' commanded the photographer. Pleased, Ella allowed the others to lift her so she lay on her side, hand propped against her cheek. Pearl took the top end. The camera snapped. They were all directed into another pose. The Cup team. Shining under the glare of fame and success. Finally, Pearl was one of them.

She looked round as the smiling silence was broken by a loud groan. Ella squatted on the ground, grasping her belly.

'You OK?' asked Pearl, crouching down beside her. Ella looked at her, closed her eyes and rocked.

'My stomach . . . It's the curse again,' she groaned. Pearl sprung back as Ella clapped her hand to her mouth and ran behind a line of orange trees. Retching sounds floated through the foliage. Dr Pond stepped forward with her medical kit.

'Did she just throw up?' grimaced Aashni. 'Proper gross.'

Pearl frowned, staring at the faint swirls of cloudiness in her Fruitogade. Something didn't smell right. And it wasn't the aroma of Ella's upset stomach. She glanced over at where Ryan stood, arms folded, by the Fruitogade table. He tipped his chin pointedly towards Jada-Rae, as if she were to blame. Pearl rolled her eyes. He wasn't being fair.

Especially as Jada-Rae now doubled over, clutching her middle. Her eyes bulged.

'I'm going to be sick too,' she groaned, before making a pained sprint through the double doors.

Pearl's head spun. Had the Fruitogade been spiked? And by whom? Jada-Rae and Ella were victims themselves. It couldn't be Coach Squibb, who crouched over his niece, looking distraught, rubbing her back gently. She studied Aashni, then Miss Cazacu, then Ryan. Supposing. Scrutinizing. Suspecting.

43

THE EXTRA SHIFTS

It was late. Jada-Rae was snoring softly but Pearl couldn't sleep. Their departure for Paris was just two nights away. She lay on her bed, staring at her phone. She dialled Dad. After a few tries, he popped up on video call, dressed in his work uniform. The picture blurred as he got out of his van and slammed the door.

'Sorry, just delivering a parcel, dumpling,' he said. He tugged his navy company cap off and ruffled his thinning hair. He looked tired.

'You're working late,' whispered Pearl, checking her watch. It was gone ten o'clock. Dad was difficult to make out in the dark.

'Ah, just doing a couple of extra shifts,' smiled Dad, like it was nothing. 'Making ends meet. I left Max with Gloria.' Pearl was quiet. She knew Dad hated to have anyone else mind Max, even Gloria. Max always cried if Dad wasn't there for lights out. Dad cleared his throat. 'So, looking forward to Paris?'

Pearl felt herself slip into lies. Well, not exactly lies, just a skirting round of so many unpleasant truths to create a totally new story. One where no one got injured, where competition was just a game and where everyone could be trusted.

Dad chatted as he got a parcel out of the back of the van and made his way up a garden path. They both paused as he rang the bell. The house owner wasn't there, so he went to leave the package with a kindly neighbour.

'Dad,' said Pearl, as he returned to the van, his phone capturing footage of the underside of his chin. Jada-Rae was still fast asleep, but Pearl ducked under the covers anyway. 'How do you know who to trust?'

Dad stopped. He leant on the side of his van. The street lights above shadowed his face.

'Not sure, dumpling. There's good in everyone, if you look hard enough. Everything OK?' Pearl batted the question away, her voice cracking. She made her excuses and hung up. Later, though, she lay awake, tossing and turning. She wished she had told him that nothing was OK at all.

44

THE SMASHED GLASS

Pearl and Jada-Rae's suitcases sat in the centre of their bunk room, neatly packed for tomorrow's journey. Next to them stood their new team rucksacks, stuffed with even newer kit. From towels, to water bottles, to travel pillows, to calming eye masks, every last thing had been provided, courtesy of Fruitogade. They were leaving early in the morning, so lights were out even before it got dark. This was it. They'd run their last morning run, showered their last lukewarm shower, eaten their last salad. It should have been a moment to celebrate – their last night at Leaping Spires. However, the mysterious stomach upsets of Ella and Jada-Rae had done something to Pearl. The fear of who might be out there, wishing ill on the gymnasts, lingered. It crept into her mind as she brushed her teeth. As she put on her pyjamas, it made her belly taut with cramps.

'Guess it's goodbye, Leaping Spires, for another year,' said Jada-Rae, slipping under her covers. 'Turn out the light, would you?'

'Actually, I've got one last goodbye to make, back in a minute,' said Pearl, hovering by the door.

'Hey, you all right?' Jada-Rae sat up, her tone soft. 'Do you want me to come?'

Pearl shook her head. This one she needed to do alone. She slipped out, bumping straight into Mrs Lulu.

'All packed for tomorrow?' smiled Mrs Lulu cheerily, wafting a gold-edged note. 'Lights out in two minutes!'

Pearl nodded and made her way to the Hall of Fame. The sun was setting. The trophies glimmered. Down the hallway was a face she wanted to take in one last time before the Cup. However, even from the doorway, she could see something was wrong.

She rushed over, taking in the sight in front of her. The floor was covered in shattered glass and broken picture frame. She crouched down slowly, picking up pieces of ripped photo from the ground, shaking off shards of glass.

She held the pieces in her hands, shaking. The photo

had been torn lengthways, then sideways, over and over, until every limb and smiling face had been severed. She picked up a crumpled scrap. *Renshu Chui – Team GB*, it read. She stepped away from the broken glass and sank down.

'Who would do this to you, Mum?' she whispered, trying to piece the photo back together. Then more quietly, 'Who would do this to me?' The sunset faded as she moved the scraps around, until only one piece was missing. The face of a girl with shiny, black hair and dimples.

She curled up in a ball, cuddling the sick feeling that she was the saboteur's new target. She gazed up at the ceiling. Was it because she had been selected? Was that why? Now she was a bigger threat? Who even knew this was her mum, except Ryan?

Suspicion slithered up the back of Pearl's neck. She shook it away. She refused to believe it. She wouldn't. She buried her face in her knees.

'Hey.' A gentle voice. A gentler nudge. Jada-Rae stood above her, looking distraught at the glassy mess. Twisting her head to take in the photo pieced together like a badly fitting jigsaw.

'That was my mum,' Pearl whispered, throat thick with tears.

Out of nowhere, Jada-Rae leant down for a hug. A really

tight, close hug. It filled Pearl with courage. Whatever it was, she had Jada-Rae on her side.

'Chupa Chup?' Never had the offer of a lollipop felt so much like kindness.

Pearl nodded, puffy-faced. Jada-Rae sat down beside her, brushing the glass out of the way.

'My secret stash. Don't tell anyone.' Pearl was not going to. She wiped her eyes. In silence, they unwrapped their lollipops.

'So, what are you going to do?' said Jada-Rae, as Pearl got through the bubblegum outer layer, and started on the lime layer. Jada-Rae seemed composed.

'What do you mean?' replied Pearl.

'Way I see it, you've got two options. One, you cry some more. Two, you ignore whoever's trying to freak you out and just smash it at the Cup.'

'How can you be so calm about this?'

'Because I know about bad things happening. I could have spent my life crying about being orphaned.' Pearl's mouth dropped open. She hadn't known Jada-Rae was an orphan. She thought of the photo in the drawer of the tall family who looked nothing like Jada-Rae. Of course.

'But that wouldn't have got me anywhere. I give myself the time it takes to eat a Chupa Chup to be sad. Then I make some choices about what I'm going to do next.

Doesn't do to be too soft, Pearl. It's a tough world and you gotta pack your heart away in a box. Otherwise, you might not make it through.'

Pearl nodded. Jada-Rae was right.

'I could cry a thousand tears every night for all my sad stories. Orphaned, boohoo. Children's home, boohoo. Foster care, boohoo. But that's not going to do anything for me.'

She finished her lolly with a crunch.

'You know what saved me? Being good at gymnastics. Everyone wants to adopt the kid who's going somewhere.'

All at once, Pearl understood Jada-Rae's drive. How being good meant safety, family and being loved. Holding her sticky lolly out of the way, she gave Jada-Rae a hug, head resting against her shoulder. The pair seemed to take a breath of sadness together, before breaking away, bonded by a new, deeper friendship that broke all Jada-Rae's rules about hearts in boxes.

45

THE EMPTY PILL PACKET

On the coach to Paris, Jada-Rae gave Pearl an earbud. Together they hummed along to their floor routine music, on repeat. By the time they reached Dover, they both knew every chord by heart. Still, all the way under the Channel, Pearl couldn't stop thinking about who was out there, waiting to do her wrong. As they sped through the darkened countryside, she pondered about stomach upsets, cloudy liquid and the torn photo. As night fell, she turned over suspects and motives in her head. After Jada-Rae asked for the hundredth time if she was all right, Pearl decided it was time to stop with the secrets.

'You know the Curse of Leaping Spires,' she said softly,

trying not to wake the others. 'It's true, but not how you think. It's not a curse, it's a somebody who keeps making bad stuff happen. They're doing anything they can to disturb the gymnasts.'

'What, like tearing up the photo of your mum?'

'And making you and Ella vomit. I think your Fruitogade was spiked.'

Jada-Rae looked out of the window at the motorway. Cars flitted by in the opposite direction under beaming street lights.

'But there's more than that. When Isla fell, it was because someone had taped a scalpel blade to the bars. When Mo fell, someone had spilt Fruitogade exactly where he normally lands. There was that time when Isla didn't perform because of itchy hands. Might have been just bad luck, but maybe it was a nasty trick. Same when all Ella's leotards were gunked up. And, of course, Zoe.'

'We can't tell anyone about this,' said Jada-Rae, her eyes wider than ever.

'Totally, except Ryan. He knows all about it.'

Jada-Rae went quiet. All the way into Paris, she tapped her fingers on the glass, thinking. They drove down the Champs-Élysées, the six lanes still streaming with traffic. They caught a glimpse of the Eiffel Tower, an illuminated triangle across the River Seine. Finally, she took Pearl's hand.

'We can't let whoever is doing this win. If we get distracted and fluff up at the Cup, they win. You promised your mum you'd win. Focus on that for her, if not for yourself.'

Pearl decided Jada-Rae was right. She squeezed her hand in agreement.

'I need the loo, I feel a bit sick again,' said Jada-Rae, rushing for the onboard toilet cubicle. Pearl looked out of the window. The coach slowed as the streets narrowed. Outside, the cafes were closing for the night. Waiters cleared away tables that spilt out on to pavements. She closed her eyes for a minute, falling into an uneasy doze.

'Hey, Pearl.'

Jada-Rae was back. Her voice was low, full of warning. She beckoned. Pearl followed her down the gangway. The team's earlier jollity had drained as the long hours of travel took their toll. Most of the gymnasts were sleeping. Jada-Rae stopped. Pearl looked over at Aashni, eyes closed, walking through her routine with tiny hand movements as she dozed. What was Jada-Rae implying? Jada-Rae shook her head and pointed on. Two rows behind, Hamish was asleep, leaning against Ella. Jada-Rae indicated further back. Ryan was snoring gently in a seat on his own. His spiky hair was crushed against the window. Jada-Rae gestured at his opened rucksack. Pearl peered in. Just in sight was a packet of pills.

Ever so carefully, Jada-Rae tipped forward and slipped her hand in. Together the girls inspected the packet.

It was empty, every pill pocket emptied. She flipped it over and read the name printed diagonally across it: Coproxol. Pearl crinkled up her nose in a question.

'It's serious pain medication. Makes you throw up if you take too many.'

Pearl's eyes widened.

'But Ryan doesn't have any injuries?' whispered Pearl. 'And he hates pill popping. Why would he have these?' Ryan stirred, frowned, then snuggled into the window.

'I think we both know, Pearl,' whispered Jada-Rae. She slipped the empty packet back into his rucksack.

'Why would he do that?' whispered Pearl, as they retraced their steps up the gangway.

'Maybe he couldn't take everyone else being better than him.'

They sat down again. The city looked darker than before.

'My mum's photo? You don't think?'

Jada-Rae sighed.

'Ryan might be your friend, but don't think he's immune to jealousy.' She offered Pearl one of her earbuds. 'We'll work it out in the morning, I need my competition sleep. So do you. Imagine, we could be podium buddies in two days' time. Think of that.'

Pearl slunk deeper in her seat. The music didn't seem inspiring any more, just empty and tinny. Soon Jada-Rae was snoring, but Pearl could not sleep. Her head spun. Was Ryan responsible for the sabotage? The mystery injuries? Had it been him the whole time? What had Ryan turned into? She thought back to before they went to Leaping Spires. Pearl could say, hand on heart, that Ryan was the most loyal friend in the world. They'd never been rivals. Though they'd trained side by side for years, Gloria had never compared them. Well, not very much anyway. Perhaps Ryan had seen it differently. Maybe he'd noticed that Gloria always worried more about him falling. That only he had to do affirmations. That his difficulty scores were always lower than hers. Was her Ryan, after all and all along, the saboteur? The one who had injured so many? If so, what should she do about it?

She shook Jada-Rae awake.

'We have to tell someone.'

Jada-Rae blinked, sandy-eyed. She nodded.

'He can't do this. As soon as we get to the hotel, we have to tell the coaches.'

As Pearl said it, she felt the last bonds of her friendship with Ryan break.

46

THE SCRAP OF PHOTO

The long curtains in Miss Cazacu's hotel suite hadn't been closed. Across the rooftops, backed by the River Seine and the orange-tinted night, stood the Fruitogade Arena, waiting for the day after tomorrow. Pearl and Jada-Rae sat awkwardly on sofas so plush their toes didn't touch the floor. Miss Cazacu was at a desk, thinking. She slowly stirred a sachet of brown sugar into her tea. Coach Squibb stood by the mantelpiece, arms crossed like a security guard. Dr Pond looked sadly out of the window, shoulders heavy with disappointment.

'You are certain about this,' said Miss Cazacu, brow furrowed. Jada-Rae and Pearl nodded.

A knock. It was Mrs Lulu, holding Ryan's rucksack. She ushered Ryan in, giving him an embarrassed smile. He hesitated, hand on the door, as he took in Pearl and Jada-Rae. Pearl felt a little part of her shrivel.

He stood in the centre of the room as Miss Cazacu began her one-woman court case. She didn't stand up. There was no need to. She was judge, jury and executioner.

'Do you know how much a top gymnast is worth?'

Ryan glanced at Pearl, questions in his eyes. Pearl looked down. Under his glasses, his eyes were so innocent, it was hard to believe he'd done what he had. Facts were facts, though.

'Do you know what the Federation has invested to turn ordinary children into winning machines?' Ryan looked around him, confused. 'We coaches aren't here for fun. We're here to create champions. With gymnastics there's a time limit on that. Once they get too grown up, their career is over. It is a sprint against time. So when I hear someone has been injuring one of my gold medal chances . . .' She pointed at Jada-Rae. 'I look poorly on it.'

Ryan looked from Pearl to Jada-Rae to Miss Cazacu to Coach Squibb to Dr Pond.

'I never . . .'

Jada-Rae raised an eyebrow.

'Empty out his bag, Mrs Lulu,' said Miss Cazacu. 'Make

yourself useful.' Mrs Lulu tipped the rucksack on to the desk, looking ashamed for Ryan. There was his audio recording equipment, a book on podcast tips and his spare glasses. However, everyone's eyes were drawn to the other objects littering the desk. Coach Squibb rushed over and held up the finished packet of Coproxol.

'You little snake,' he growled. 'You poisoned Ella, didn't you?'

'And me,' butted in Jada-Rae.

'I've never seen those before, I promise,' said Ryan, stepping back from Coach Squibb's quivering moustache.

'What's this?' said Miss Cazacu. She picked up a scrap of photo delicately, as if she were handling a butterfly wing. It was the missing piece of Mum's photo, torn halfway down her dimples. Pearl curled her fists. *How could he? He deserved everything he got.*

'He vandalized her mum's photo,' blurted out Jada-Rae, taking Pearl's hand.

'I didn't!' cried Ryan, shaking his head vigorously. 'I wouldn't! She's my – she was my—'

'Of course,' Miss Cazacu interrupted, looking at Pearl. 'You're Renshu's daughter.' Her expression was unreadable.

'That's where they went,' said Dr Pond, coming over from the window. She picked up the injury files Pearl had stolen, now heavily annotated in Ryan's handwriting.

'I suspected someone had been stealing from my room. Miss Cazacu, can we really have thieves on the team?'

'But . . .' yelled Ryan, gripping his head in panic. 'Pearl? Tell them!'

Ryan looked at her, desperation in his eyes. She couldn't admit she stole the files, though. What if she got kicked off the Cup team? Anyway, he was the saboteur, even if he was telling the truth about the files.

Miss Cazacu lasered Pearl with a hard stare. Jada-Rae shook her head. Pearl returned Miss Cazacu's look.

'There's nothing to tell.'

At that, Ryan closed his mouth. He didn't speak another word.

'You are a thief, a vandal and a saboteur,' said Miss Cazacu. 'Shame on you. If only you'd spent the time improving your difficulty scores.'

'Do you wish to call his parents? Have him sent home?' suggested Mrs Lulu politely. 'Perhaps the girls should step outside?'

Jada-Rae got up to go. Pearl's heart strained, thinking of Gloria's voice as she answered the phone.

Miss Cazacu raised a single finger. 'No, parents make trouble. The sponsors will not want that. If the papers run stories, it is a disaster. Especially so close to an event. We will drop him after the Cup.' Ryan looked winded. 'Until then he must be kept away from the other gymnasts. Mrs Lulu, since your duties are a little less involved than the rest of the staff' – Mrs Lulu's nostrils flared at the casual insult – 'you are responsible for his supervision. Keep him in the other bedroom of that surprisingly generous corner suite you've taken. No familiarization session. No team meals. Understood?' Mrs Lulu nodded, her face unsmiling.

'Dr Pond, Coach Squibb – at the Cup, keep him on the shortest of leashes.' Dr Pond nodded gravely. Coach Squibb smiled unpleasantly.

As Pearl followed Jada-Rae out of the room, she didn't dare catch Ryan's eye. Though she was totally in the right, she had a bitter taste in her mouth – the taste of betrayal.

47

THE GOLDEN NOTEBOOK

The lift was as old as the hotel, perhaps older. Its cables creaked as it approached. Above its doors, illuminated numbers charted its sluggish progress. Five . . . six . . . The sounds of the lobby spiralled up the stairwell beside them. No one spoke. Mrs Lulu and Coach Squibb stood on either side of Ryan, as if he might make a run for it at any moment. Ryan stayed perfectly still. The backs of his ears burnt a resentful red, as if signalling his views on Pearl to her. Pearl hung back with Jada-Rae, wishing the swirly patterned carpet would swallow her up.

Ping! Floor seven. The lift arrived with a *thunk*. Its doors opened squeakily. Inside stood a middle-aged man with a greying beard. Pearl gasped. It was the man she and Ryan had spied dropping off Miss Cazacu in the car park at Leaping Spires. He wore a tracksuit with a blue, yellow and red striped flag on the chest. Taking them in, he gave a small snort. He looked surprised to see so many people so late in the evening. Coach Squibb crossed his arms. Mrs Lulu twitched in recognition. They stood back to let him through. He passed, awkwardly avoiding eye contact.

'Thought you'd asked for separate hotels from the other teams,' grumbled Coach Squibb as they crammed in the lift. 'Especially from the coach of our greatest rivals.' His nostrils flared in dislike. Pearl bunched up close to Jada-Rae. The air felt stifling. The lift sign read: *Seulement 4 personnes*. The lift groaned.

'I did,' huffed Mrs Lulu. 'I'll let Miss Cazacu know the Romanians are sniffing around again.' Of course, the flag on his tracksuit was Romanian. Pearl had seen it countless times on her poster of the young Elena Cazacu.

Squashed in the corner, Ryan looked pointedly at Pearl.

'Actually, I'll take the stairs,' said Pearl. She stepped out.

'Race you,' smiled Jada-Rae, pressing the lift button. She waved as its doors closed on them. Pearl waved weakly in return, turning for the stairwell. She exhaled, able to breathe again. She couldn't be in a small space with Ryan. Saboteur or not, he had been her best friend. Always there for her, always training together. When she'd heard the news about Mum, he'd sat for hours with her, while she just stared out of the window. He'd never let her down. Until now.

Down the corridor, the man with the greying beard was kneeling, tying his shoelace slowly. It was as if he was waiting for the corridor to clear. Pearl took a step down the stairs. She paused. What had Ryan's look meant? A thought occurred to her. She crept back up the stairs. Pressing her hands to the wall, she peeked down the corridor.

The man was knocking at Miss Cazacu's door. He stood back, waiting. Out of his pocket, he pulled a notebook. The golden notebook that held every last training secret of Leaping Spires. Pearl put her hand to her mouth. The door opened.

'Zoltan! And did I forget my notebook? Silly me.' Miss Cazacu broke into Romanian, her voice warm and friendly, different to how she spoke to the gymnasts. Pearl jerked back. Her head swirled. She stumbled down the flights of stairs, grabbing the banisters, her balance escaping her. Was Miss Cazacu a mole? Passing information back to her old team? If Miss Cazacu would betray her own team, what else might she do to them? A moment ago, Pearl had been so sure Ryan was guilty. Now doubt wormed up her spine. By the time she reached her floor, she felt panicky.

'Hey, I won!' Jada-Rae stood, arms raised in victory. Her smile was wide and carefree.

'What?' said Pearl, heart aching for a friend, someone with whom to share what she'd just seen.

'Our race, remember?' said Jada-Rae, dropping her arms. 'You all right, buddy?'

'You don't think Miss Cazacu is a mole, do you? For the Romanians?'

Jada-Rae looked stunned. She stuttered before shaking the thought away.

'N-no, not possible. She wouldn't.' She took Pearl's cheeks in her hands, her eyes full of concern.

'You're letting what's happened get to you. It's only one day until the Cup. That's all you should be thinking about now.' Her face transformed into a wide smile. 'Want to walk through our routines in my room?'

Pearl nodded. Jada-Rae's constant sunniness was incredible. She had never let the sabotage get to her, not really. She hadn't got upset when they'd suspected Ryan. She didn't get paranoid about snooping rival coaches. She just focused on winning. This was how Pearl needed to act to be a true champion. Unemotional, undistractable, unstoppable. Made of a tougher fibre. And yet, was that the kind of champion Mum would have wanted her to be?

48

THE OTHER COACH

Sixteen hours, twenty minutes and ten seconds to go. In the Fruitogade Arena, the longest hand ticked on a huge clock, counting down each second until the competition. Rows of stadium seating watched every angle of the oval performance area. At one end, a giant scoreboard waited to be lit up with names and scores. An empty VIP box sat halfway up the stands, ready for tomorrow's dignitaries. The gymnasts were scattered across their chosen apparatus, quiet with focus. They only had thirty minutes to familiarize themselves with the equipment before tomorrow. It was like everyone was preparing for the greatest exam of all time. The last rehearsal.

On the beam, Pearl practised her weakest connections, trying to keep focused. The pressure hung lifeless in the air, crushing all the fun.

She glanced across at the pommel, the rings and the parallel bars, half-expecting to see Ryan with the boys. However, he was not. Excluded. Untrusted. It felt strange Ryan not being there and even weirder to think of him held in a hotel room, while she prepared for the biggest competition of both of their lives. They had always competed together, side by side in their successes and failures. Until now. It made no sense, especially as she had a new suspect with a darker motive. She stretched back into a backwards walkover.

'You did not say you were Renshu's daughter.' Miss Cazacu had appeared at the end of the beam. It was unclear if this was an accusation.

Pearl righted herself, pausing her routine. She stared at Miss Cazacu. The bird-like frame. The short, fair crop. The gold eyeshadow shimmering over pale blue eyes. The golden notebook, that only last night she'd seen a rival coach returning. If she was a mole for the Romanians, it would have been so easy for her to conduct the sabotage. After all, everyone idolized her, Mum especially. She'd said Miss Cazacu taught her to believe in herself.

'What was my mum like, as a gymnast?' she asked.

Miss Cazacu studied her, as if weighing something up in her mind.

'She glittered with gold. I see her in you now. Same smile. Same lift in your toes. You will make her proud tomorrow. And me.' She said it with a finality, like it was already decided.

Could she be innocent? Pearl longed for a coach who believed she glittered with gold, supporting her just as Mum had. Not one who sabotaged her own gymnasts. Yet if Miss Cazacu was guilty, was Ryan innocent?

Session over, the team made their way the two blocks back from the arena to the hotel. They walked four abreast, weaving around cafe tables being packed away. They passed pastry shops and expensive boutiques closing for the night. Jada-Rae greeted passers-by in French. Ella livestreamed everything. Even Aashni looked impressed by the chic Parisians. However, Pearl couldn't stop thinking about Miss Cazacu, Ryan and the Cup tomorrow.

Her phone rang. The caller ID read simply: *COACH*. She prised herself out of her team-mates' arms, waving them on.

'Pearl!' Gloria's voice sounded relieved. 'How are you? How's Paris? Seen the Eiffel Tower yet?' Then: 'Have you spoken to Ryan?'

'No,' said Pearl. Truthfully.

'He's not returning my calls. Can you get him to call me? Makes me worried when he doesn't call. Too busy being a superstar gymnast, I guess.' Pearl thought she heard Gloria's voice crack.

'Gloria,' said Pearl. She had to tell her what had happened. Gloria was quiet as Pearl explained: about Zoe, Mo and Isla, the poisoning, the torn photo, and about Ryan not saying a word as he was accused.

When Pearl stopped, Gloria's reaction was so loud it made a passing old lady jump. A little dog yapped in shock.

'I can't believe Miss Cazacu kept this from me, but I expected more from you. Have you gone totally daft? Sabotage? Injuries? What did he do all that for, so he could talk about it on his podcast? You think my son did it? He's your oldest mate! He's spent a lifetime being there to catch you.' She made it seem so simple. So obvious. 'He'd never do that to Renshu either. She never trained him to be a cheat.'

Pearl caught her reflection in a pastry shop window. Beside a stack of macarons was a girl full of foolishness. She hadn't really considered that Ryan was a product of Mum's coaching – drilled in being fair and honest.

Gloria softened at Pearl's silence. 'Pearl, I don't know what's being going on there, but you need to be careful. I don't believe for a second Ryan is capable of any of that, which means someone else is. I just wish I could talk to him. Can't you go and see him?' Her voice wavered. 'I'm sure this could all be sorted out with a chat, Pearl. You've got to give him that, at least. Bagley End Butterflies have to stick together.'

Pearl hung up. She thought of Ryan spotting her tumbles, session after session, knees bent, arms raised. With him, she always dared to flip higher, knowing he would catch her if she fell. Her lungs curled with misgiving. She glanced up the street at the vanishing gymnasts and staff. Was the saboteur Miss Cazacu? She couldn't quite believe it. However, one person she just knew it couldn't be was the boy stuck in a hotel room under supervision at all times. Her best friend in the world – Ryan.

49

THE OPENED LAPTOP

Mrs Lulu stood in the doorway of her first-floor corner suite, smiling expectantly at Pearl. Her evening attire was even brighter than her daywear – a hot-pink kimono with a swishing trail. The familiar melody of the 'Overture from the Barber of Seville' played out of an open laptop she was holding. Behind her, evening light streamed across the lounge, bathing the sofas in an orange glow. On the far side were two identical doors. Behind one of them was Ryan, watched like a criminal, while all along the true saboteur laughed.

'Well, this is a nice surprise, Pearl. I was just checking your floor music for tomorrow. I'm coordinating all the music for our girls' routines. Can't be mixing up these audio files! How can I help? Last-minute leotard alteration, I'm guessing?'

'Can I speak to Ryan?'

Mrs Lulu pressed pause on her laptop abruptly. Her smile disappeared.

'It's your big day tomorrow. You should be minimizing distractions. Let's leave the visits for another time.'

'Just five minutes in private.' Pearl crossed her arms stubbornly, Gloria's words echoing in her mind.

'I'm sorry, I'm under strict instructions. Our young saboteur can't see anyone.' She smiled sympathetically, readjusting her grip on her laptop.

'He's not . . .' Pearl began. Seeing a twitch on Mrs Lulu's lips, she stopped. Mrs Lulu didn't want to know. No one wanted to hear that the saboteur might not be Ryan. The matter had been solved, neatly. The staff had never really rooted for Ryan or thought he was a true winner anyway.

'Ryan!' Pearl shouted. 'Ryan!' Mrs Lulu reared up. There was a coldness in her eyes that made Pearl squirm. Behind her, one of the doors opened. Ryan stood in it, eating a room service pudding. Their eyes met. He looked full of hurt.

'I'm sorry,' Pearl called across the room.

Ryan nodded, looking down at his pudding plate.

'Enough now, Pearl.' Mrs Lulu smiled icily. Balancing

her opened laptop in one hand, she went to close the door. Pearl put her foot in the way.

'Will you help me?' she called.

Ryan just kept studying his plate, like it contained the secrets to the universe. Pearl realized a terrible thing. Friendships are fragile and must be protected, because once broken, they can't always be fixed. She held on for a moment but there was nothing more she could say.

'I'll go now.'

Mrs Lulu nodded and shut the door gently. Pearl made her way back down the corridor, stopping at the stairwell window, willing Ryan to somehow slip out after her. He didn't.

She looked down the empty street. One block down, a slight figure in a team hoodie slipped towards the arena. Was it a gymnast, or maybe Miss Cazacu?

The blood rushed in Pearl's ears. Her head throbbed. She clenched her fists, squeezing deep into her callused palms. For the first time since Mum had got sick, she felt an uncontrollable anger. The saboteur had turned her gymnastic dream into a night terror of broken bones. They had stood in the shadows while Pearl betrayed her best friend. They had made fair play feel as fanciful as happy endings. She turned and sprinted down the stairs. This time the saboteur wasn't getting away with it.

50

THE OPEN WINDOW

Pearl crouched behind a barricade. Ahead of her, the Fruitogade Arena gleamed in the setting sun. It was not going to be easy to break into. Security was high. Competitors and supporters were long gone for the day. Guards were ushering out the last of the cleaners. For the saboteur, this would be the perfect time to mess with the apparatus. She watched a security guard lock the door and walk away, loosening his tie.

'Excuse me!' Pearl bobbed up from behind the barricade. He stopped. 'Excuse me,' said Pearl again, rushing up. 'Did you see anyone go back in? My coach, maybe?'

The guard looked her up and down.

'No adults. Just a girl who forgot her gym bag.'

'What did she look like?' asked Pearl, frowning. Had she been wrong about Miss Cazacu?

'Smaller than you. In a hoodie.' This didn't tell Pearl much. All the gymnasts were shorter than her and they all had a regulation hoodie.

'Did you see her leave?' said Pearl, trailing after the guard as he headed to a security booth.

'I did not see. But *oui*! She must have.' He said this with the finality of a man who was done talking to a twelve-year-old after a long day on his feet. He unlocked the door to the booth and sat himself down in front of the security cameras. He tapped his phone, conversation finished.

Pearl made her way around the side of the building. It was all most definitely locked up. However, if the saboteur was inside, she needed to find a way in. She checked a fire exit door. Nope. Another. It was all secure. She sighed, looking up. Sunset reflected on copper panels. She shielded her eyes. Attached to the wall of the building hung the Olympic rings. Five interlinked circles, a symbol that made every aspiring athlete's heart skip a beat. As the daylight faded, they flickered into life. The neon tubes illuminated in blue, black, red, yellow and green. Above them, Pearl noticed a small window ajar. It was a way in. It was also three metres up.

Pearl walked away from the building. She turned around. Out of habit, she made a salute to no one in particular. Then began her run-up. Feet padding on tarmac. Getting faster. Sprinting. She leapt, as if to catch imaginary uneven bars. She sailed up and forward. Her hands caught the bottom Olympic ring. She pushed her feet forward to cushion her impact against the wall, knees crunching into her chest. A twist inside the bottom ring. A worrying wobble.

Pearl tried not to think about the lack of crash mat below her feet as she pulled herself into the opening. Her tracksuit caught on the window fastening as she wormed her way through. She wiggled, but it wouldn't come free. For a moment she stilled herself, half-in, half-out of the building. Then propelled herself forward. Her tracksuit sheared at the back as she wrenched it free.

Pearl landed in a heap on her weaker ankle on slippy tiles. She looked around. She was in the toilets. The boys' toilets. It smelt of wee masked with bleach. She got to her feet, testing out her ankle. Thankfully, it was OK. The corridor outside was wide and deathly quiet, curving round the edge of the arena. She sneaked along, checking behind her. She peered through the window panel of a door into the main arena. Rows of empty seats faced down to the gymnastics area. The sunset was stealing out through high windows, leaving darkness behind. Pearl slipped in.

She crept down, careful not to disturb the stillness. Leaning on the barrier at the bottom, she looked across the dark shapes of the gymnastic apparatus and the main floor display square. It was entirely empty. Or was it?

On the near side of the gymnastics area, only a few paces away, was a small figure in a hoodie, a rucksack on their back. They were standing at the end of the vault run, sprinkling something into a chalk bowl. The figure glanced around, then moved to the next apparatus. Again, they stopped, sprinkled something into the chalk bowl. Pearl hesitated. This was the saboteur. No question.

'Hey!' Pearl called, squinting into the dark. The person started, backflipping away with the force of an opposing magnet. The backflip looked strangely familiar. Pearl leapt over the barrier and into the performance area. A sprint forward, a handspring up on to the performance platform. A look ahead to direct herself. There. A shadow tumbled away. Pearl cartwheeled after them, covering ground at dizzying speed. The shadow was heading for the main exit.

'Wait!' However, the shadow would not wait. They double backflipped straight across the floor area. A leap over the barrier. A dash to the exit doors. The figure shook the closed doors. They rattled, but did not budge. Whoever it was, was locked in.

Slowly, steadily, her stomach curling, Pearl climbed over the barrier and approached.

'Jada-Rae?'

51

THE GLITTER OF GOLD

The gymnasts stood facing each other in the dark. Two slight silhouettes in an empty arena, separated by the distance of a backflip or two.

'Oh, hey!' said Jada-Rae. Her voice was relaxed, as if they were sharing popcorn on a Saturday night.

'It was you,' whispered Pearl, as much to herself as to Jada-Rae. 'You sabotaged your own squad mates? Zoe? Ella? Isla?'

'I didn't think she'd fall that badly.'

'Mo? Thought you liked him?'

'That one wasn't me,' muttered Jada-Rae.

'Mum's photo?'

'Not me either.'

Pearl laughed coldly.

'You sabotaged my vault, didn't you? You faked your Fruitogade being spiked.'

Jada-Rae snorted but didn't deny it.

'We were friends.'

'It wasn't personal.'

Jada-Rae cartwheeled across the dim arena towards Pearl. Pearl stepped back. Danger hung in the air. She twisted, hurdling over the beam – creating a barrier between Jada-Rae and her.

'Look, this isn't just survival of the fittest. It's survival of the toughest.' Jada-Rae's voice was as soft as marshmallow. She moved towards the beam, circling around it as Pearl moved the other way.

'To win, you've got to be prepared to cut down the competition. By whatever means necessary. Be that injuries, psyching them out, unlucky falls or unfortunate stomach upsets.'

She leapt up on to the beam, towering over Pearl. A final shard of sunset from the high windows cut across her eyes. They flashed with triumph. Something seemed to shuffle high in the stands. Jada-Rae froze for a second, giving Pearl a chance to advance on the beam. She leapt up on the far end. Eye-level now, but out of grabbing distance.

'You're not going to win. I'm going straight to Miss Cazacu.'

A laugh. Jada-Rae's famous cackle. Now it sounded hard, humourless.

'You don't know, do you?' she said, tiptoeing down the beam. Pearl didn't like how close she was getting. She leapt down, guessing her landing in the dark.

'Who do you think encouraged me to do this? Miss Cazacu doesn't care. None of them do. Not about you or any other gymnast I've taken out.'

She did a handspring down, landing centimetres away. She was so close Pearl could feel her breath.

'She just wants to see gymnasts that will survive on the Olympic pathway.' Pearl took a step back.

'In me, Miss Cazacu sees grit.' She shoved Pearl's chest. 'Determination.' A harder push. Pearl stumbled back. 'And a heart of steel.' Pearl jumped to avoid another shove, knocking over a chalk bowl stand as she tripped. Chalk sprayed across her as she lay starfished out. It got in her eyes, her nose, her mouth.

'When she says "win at all costs", she means it. She trained me to be like this,' continued Jada-Rae.

Pearl scrambled up, dusting off chalk, coughing as she retreated. She needed to get away before she was really hurt. Jada-Rae's voice rang in her ears.

'So if you mess with her best chance of Olympic success – do you think it'll be me off the team? Or you, with your pathetic low-scoring half-twists and your sloppy "club gymnastics" techniques? Especially with no proof at all.'

Pearl blinked away the chalk dust stinging her eyes.

'I don't believe you,' she gasped.

'We both know you do.'

Pearl didn't reply, glancing behind her at the dark lines of the uneven bars. She felt like she was carrying a boulder in her heart, because she knew Jada-Rae was right. No one would listen. No one would believe her. There was no one to tell.

'Now, would you like to medal tomorrow or not?'

Pearl stepped backwards. The uneven bars were directly above her. Jada-Rae cartwheeled forward.

'I always know I'm the winner. Before I walk out into the arena, I've already won.' Her voice softened. 'You can medal too, Pearl. Like I said, none of this is personal. I actually like you. I can make it happen.'

Pearl did a standing jump up, catching the bar. She swung backwards and forwards, warding Jada-Rae off with her feet.

'This is our moment, Pearl. You and me. We'll be on the podium together. I'll take gold. You take silver. Imagine that.'

She was close now. Pearl could see the white glint of her teeth as she talked. Pearl twisted and swung up on to the high bar.

'We'll be a team. Us against the world. We can cut down everyone in the Cup tomorrow. And then one day the Olympics.' The possibility hung in the darkened space in a fine mist. It could work. Guaranteed winning. Pearl spun up and then released, landing further from Jada-Rae.

'Come on,' said Jada-Rae, her voice kind. 'You said you wanted to shine brightly, do your mum proud. Make some sense of losing her. That's what you told me. You could finally make her dream come true.'

Pearl keeled over, like she'd been punched. How could she have ever told Jada-Rae her most trusted secret – one she'd never even told Ryan?

Up in the stands, something clattered. A plastic seat flipping. The girls paused. Silence returned. Pearl straightened up.

'You're right, Jada-Rae. I do want to make my mum proud. And I am going to make her dreams come true. I'm going to win tomorrow. But without you and your cheating. I'm going to win the right way.'

An alarm sounded in the building. Pearl put her hands to her ears, eyes darting to the green exit light. A fist grabbed her tracksuit at the front, yanking it so it tore more. Jada-Rae eyeballed her, reducing her voice to a whisper.

'I like you, Pearl, but I'm going to win tomorrow. And if you get in my way, you'll end up in an ambulance. Like the rest of them.'

She slipped into the shadows, disappearing like falling sand. The exit door clacked open and closed. She was gone. Pearl was left with a mouth clagging with chalk, a ripped tracksuit and a thumping in her head, because she knew what tomorrow would bring.

52

THE DIRECTIONAL MICROPHONE

Night had fallen outside the arena. The street was in shadow. Pearl picked her way back to the hotel, winding around the light of the street lamps. She checked behind her again. Was someone following her? It was hard to tell in the dark. The moon peered out behind clouds, hunting for secrets and lurkers. Frightened, she sped up. She broke into a run. A sprint. Lungs exploding, she reached the corner of the hotel. She had to find Ryan. Beg him. Anything. Before whoever was following got to her.

She looked up at the first-floor corner balcony. It was the height of a high bar. Too far to jump. She needed to reach Ryan, though. She eyed a metal drainpipe running up to the balcony. She darted over to it. Channelling every rope climb she'd ever done, she gripped the slippery metal. She shimmied up at speed. If someone was following her, hopefully they couldn't keep up. She leant across, catching the edge of the balcony. Legs trembling, she hoisted herself over the metalwork. She felt along until she found the French windows ajar. Scuffing sounded below. She slipped inside.

'Ryan?'

No answer. Next door, Mrs Lulu was playing a waltz, Ella's floor piece. Pearl crept up to the shadowed bed.

'Wake up.' Pearl looked at the boy-shaped lump under the duvet. 'I was wrong. You're my best friend. You always were.' She prodded the duvet. It squished down. There was no one in the bed.

A scratching came from the balcony. Pearl dropped to the floor and flattened herself down. Whoever it was, was slipping into the hotel suite.

'Pearl?' said a cuddly-shaped silhouette holding a directional microphone. Relief shook through Pearl as she jumped up.

'Ryan, I've so much to tell you,' she whispered.

'I know.'

The music stopped. The two stepped closer. A wild

drumming began as Mrs Lulu checked Aashni's rock track next door.

'Jada-Rae's the saboteur,' whispered Pearl. 'She has been all along. Miss Cazacu's involved too.'

'I know,' said Ryan, putting down his audio equipment.

'Why do you keep saying "I know"?' said Pearl, as loudly as she dared.

'Because I followed you, silly. You said you wanted help.'

Pearl was filled with an unusual urge to hug Ryan, but he wasn't the hugging type.

'What are we going to do now? Tell Mrs Lulu?'

Ryan shook his head. 'She does whatever Miss Cazacu says. We can't trust her.'

'Then what?'

For once, all her positivity had dried up. She just felt small and scared. Ryan took off his glasses, rubbing them on the edge of his top. He put them back on, as if armouring himself.

'Tomorrow, you're going to do the performance of your life.' He paused. 'And so . . . am I. Doing it the right way. I'll have your back; you'll have mine. Then once you've beaten Jada-Rae, the world will want to know what a cheat she is.' The moonlight glanced over his face. Pearl saw a look she hadn't seen on him for a long while. A look of conviction.

'Oh, before I forget.' He rummaged through his suitcase. 'I couldn't let you throw this away.'

He handed Pearl something light blue and soft. Her old leotard. She smiled, stroking the fabric. She would always be a Bagley End Butterfly. Pearl looked at Ryan. She would always have his back.

'I know it's too small for you now,' said Ryan. 'But your mum made it, so I thought you could at least keep it for the memories.'

'Thank you, Ryan,' said Pearl.

Jada-Rae's floor piece, 'The Blue Danube', began to play next door. They hastily agreed a plan.

'Are you sure it will work?' questioned Pearl, as Ryan helped her over the metalwork of the balcony.

'Trust me,' said Ryan. For the first time in forever, he looked and sounded like he really believed in himself.

Pearl looked down, assessing the drop to the pavement. She swung down, landing softly, knees bent. She raised her arms in a salute for luck. Tomorrow, they would become champions, together. Then she dropped her arms, frowning. She had a suspicion it wouldn't be as easy as that.

53

THE UNFURLED BANNER

Miss Cazacu led the eight gymnasts out of the changing rooms in silence. Ryan was at the back, flanked by Coach Squibb and Dr Pond. As they stepped into the arena, the sound of the crowd hit Pearl like a wall. Clapping and cheering echoed from the stands. National flags were everywhere, draped over shoulders, made into banners and painted on cheeks. The smell of coffee and croissants wafted down from pop-up carts. Cameras flashed. On the competition floor, gymnasts in shiny national tracksuits jogged up and down tumble tracks, ignoring the camera crews. Arena staff checked equipment. Up in the VIP area, the sponsors tucked into a complimentary buffet. Beside them in the audio booth, Mrs Lulu waved, already standing by with the music for the team's routines. Pearl twitched with tension and lack of sleep.

They walked round the edge of the competition area, passing coaches giving gymnasts pep talks and physios doing last-minute shoulder rubs. Pearl read the printed boards laid out along the edges. There were three-letter abbreviations for each country. FRA, GER, HUN, ROM, NED, USA. And at the end, GBR. Their designated team area. She slung her bag down under their bench and took a seat, trying to keep calm. Aashni sat beside her, jiggling her knees, staring straight ahead, chewing gum, headphones on. Ella was at the end, adding extra hair gel to her slicked-back fringe. She took a final, smiling selfie, before slipping into an anxious frown. Jada-Rae took the spare place by Pearl. She hummed to her music, as if she had no care in the world. Ryan glanced over. Pearl avoided his eye. She stood up. She couldn't be near Jada-Rae.

Then it was time. The four rotations were starting and her first event was floor. Pearl unzipped her torn tracksuit, revealing her new leotard for the first time in competition. She flexed her shoulders back, the silky-smooth green fabric catching the light. Pearls gleamed down her sleeves. Mum's lucky leotard was packed away safely, but it was

OK. A tiny part of Mum was still layered tightly all around her, willing her on. She returned to the bench and squatted down to put her tracksuit away. Jada-Rae moved her feet to the side. Aashni gave Pearl a surly thumbs up. Ella smiled and crossed both her fingers.

'Hey, good luck,' added Jada-Rae with the nicest smile possible, glancing down at Pearl's bag.

Pearl hardened her jaw. She unzipped her bag, which lay just beside Jada-Rae's feet. She rummaged through. However, nothing had been touched. For now. She stuffed her tracksuit in. She would not be beaten by mind games.

She looked at Jada-Rae, trying to keep her eyes unnarrowed.

'I don't need luck today,' Pearl said evenly. Only a tiny shake in her voice gave her away.

'We'll see,' whispered Jada-Rae.

'Pearl!'

Up in the stands there was a commotion. A burly man in a navy uniform, a woman with short curls and a scruffy-haired boy were hurrying down the steps. A giant banner trailed after them. Pearl's heart leapt into her mouth.

Dad never came to competitions. That was always Mum's thing. Until today. He had come all the way to Paris, bringing Max and Gloria.

Pearl watched them unfurl the banner. *Go, Bagley End Butterflies!* it read. She turned and waved. They flipped the banner round. *We LOVE you!*

Max bounded to the bottom of the stand steps. He leant over the barriers, waving madly. Pearl ran across for a hug.

'Missed you,' he said, giving her a big, wet kiss.

'Max, if I get hurt, tell Dad I love him.' She kissed his messy hair, squeezing him tight.

'Why would you get hurt?' said Max, face knotting with confusion.

Pearl smiled tightly and made her way to the competition mat. Knowing all the people who loved her were up in the crowd made her feel stronger. Yet the fear of what might go wrong on the gymnastics floor seemed to triple before her eyes.

54

THE WHITE POWDER

In the corner of the floor square, Pearl swivelled into her starting pose. The green light illuminated. Up in the sound booth, Mrs Lulu, made a thumbs up sign. The crowd hushed as 'Overture from the Barber of Seville' began. Pulse already pounding, she was off. Every twist was tight. Every shape was strong. Powered by love, she was going to perform. The presence of Dad, Max and Gloria in the stands catapulted her forward. The gaze of Ryan from the benches steadied her landings. She felt like she was flying, each chord propelling her up into her next tumble. When she finished, her scores lit up the stadium. The best performance of her life. Shining on a bigger stage than ever before.

As she took her seat, waiting for her next event, her stomach churned at what Jada-Rae was planning. She looked over at the vault. Jada-Rae had scattered sugar on her springboard back at Leaping Spires, but she couldn't do that so easily here. Not with so many officials watching.

Pearl went to take a sip of water, then put the bottle down. She couldn't be sure Jada-Rae hadn't tampered with it. She stretched her shoulders back, trying to squeeze the worries away. She stood up, shaking herself out, watching the other competitors on vault.

A French girl was finishing her routine. She landed arms raised, then walked off the mats, shaking her head and scratching her hands.

Pearl made her way to the end of the vault runway. She glanced around, scanning for Jada-Rae. She went to dip her hands in the chalk bowl. Then stopped. The texture of the chalk was less fine at the top. This was the same chalk bowl she'd seen Jada-Rae sprinkling something into. She remembered Isla's complaint about itchy hands after her floor assessment, weeks ago. Was it itching powder? Pearl couldn't risk it. It would be a no-chalk routine.

Pearl raised her arms in salute for the first of her two vault runs. Her hands were already sweating. She ran, legs pumping, lungs bursting. On to the springboard, feet together, landing bang on in the centre. Pushing off strongly. Her hands pressed firmly into the vaulting table, shoulders square. She flipped up.

Spinning. Spinning.

She landed.

With a hop.

A strong performance, but not perfect. One tenth deduction for the extra hop. One more vault to go. She walked back, checking her hands. She glanced over to the benches. Jada-Rae sat there. She made a sympathetic face. Pearl looked away. In a few strides and under five seconds in the air, her chances of winning could disappear. There was no room for anything but perfection.

Salute. Sprint. Leap. Push off. Flip.

Spinning. Spinning.

She landed within the lines, feet together.

She crunched small, then unfurled. She had performed.

She returned to the benches, lungs pounding. As she waited for her next event, the other scores came in. The Romanians hadn't performed well, the French were off their game and the Germans had executed poorly. Aashni and Ella were way down, behind the Russians. Pearl was in second place. This was brilliant, except that she was behind the one girl she refused to be beaten by: Jada-Rae Williams.

55

THE STICKY GRIPS

Pearl sat waiting. She drummed her fingers on her thighs, jumpy with nerves. Jada-Rae got up for her next event, giving Pearl a sickly smile. Pearl didn't return it. She knew those smiles were worth nothing now.

'Next contestant, Pearl Bolton,' called an announcer through the PA system. Pearl picked up her hand grips.

'No!'

Along the bench, Aashni and Ella looked up. They gasped. Pearl's leather hand grips, worn smooth with practice, were smeared with something slippy. Wet. A sticky splurge of chewing gum. It had been wiped across the dowels, and into the inside too. The gooey, grey strands clumped into the pores. Aashni paused, mid-chew, taking off her headphones. Then stopped chewing, knowing how guilty she looked.

'It wasn't me,' she mumbled.

'I know,' replied Pearl, chucking the grips down furiously. How could she perform with sticky grips? They'd glue her to the bar, slowing her releases and sticking up her catches.

'Then who?' said Aashni. She grabbed a grip and began picking off the blobs of gum in a frenzy. Ella raced round to take the other grip. She scratched at the gum. It wasn't coming off. It just stretched into a sticky mess. Aashni paused. She twisted round to face Ella.

'Was it you?'

Ella shook her head, her princess buns quivering.

'Was it your uncle, then?' snorted Aashni. She pointed over at Coach Squibb. He stood, hands on hips, watching his boys' performances intently.

Ella blushed guiltily.

'Jada-Rae just told me. Kept that secret, didn't you?' seethed Aashni. 'Was this another of his ways to help you win?' She returned a grip to Pearl, the gum still smeared everywhere.

'No!' Ella shook her head fiercely. 'He wouldn't do this. I wouldn't either.' She returned Pearl's other gummed-up grip.

'I know,' said Pearl gently. 'I know who would though.' She looked over at where Jada-Rae was sprinting for the vault. Ella and Aashni followed her look, slowly understanding.

'Her?' whispered Aashni.

'How could she?' gulped Ella. She dived for her own dainty hand grips. 'Borrow mine.'

'Or mine,' suggested Aashni, pushing hers into Pearl's hands. 'My hands are more your size.'

'Last call. Pearl Bolton on bars,' the announcer repeated.

'Thank you, Aashni,' Pearl said. She would tell them both everything that had happened when there was enough time. 'Really, I'm—'

'Just go!' cried Ella. 'Win for us!'

As Pearl sprinted to the bars, she understood why Mum had always talked so fondly of her team-mates from Leaping Spires. And how she loved her gymnastics friendships as much as gymnastics itself.

Pearl arrived breathlessly at the uneven bars. She hurriedly saluted the judges. Miss Cazacu stepped forward to assist, twitching at Pearl's lack of punctuality. She pursed her lips at Pearl's lightning-patterned, badly fitting grips. Pearl ignored her. She didn't need the approval of a woman who would sabotage her own team. All she needed was to do a

G.O.A.T. performance. Pearl Bolton, Greatest Of All Time. Or at least, greatest of the International Cup.

'Go on, Pearl,' called a honeyed voice. Jada-Rae was passing, returning from her event. She unwrapped a stick of chewing gum slowly and popped it in her mouth. The cruelty of it spurred Pearl on.

She focused on the bars ahead. One, two, three, four, five steps, on to the springboard and up. Miss Cazacu pulled the springboard out of the way and stood back. Pearl swung upside down. Her grips tugged, rubbing uncomfortably and causing her to misalign. She corrected, refusing to be put off, then dived into an upstart. She rose up then released, flying through the air like a bird. She caught the high bar perfectly, but as she curled her fingers in, the rubbing increased. She ignored it and soared up into a handstand. She reversed her hands, one after another. A second holding her pose. The arena faded into the background as she descended into a forward giant. She swung outstretched round the bar and released. She flew through the air. Twisting, flipping. She caught the low bar cleanly. A pain shot through her as her calluses ripped. Her hands screamed as the skin tore, but she had to keep going. She circled the bar, building up to the one positive trick Jada-Rae had taught her. The full-out dismount. She curled, spun and twisted, landing cleanly.

She walked back to her seat, eyeing the scoreboard, hands trickling with blood. As her number came up she heard whoops across the arena from Gloria, Max and Dad. There, on the top of the scoreboard, was her name. Way ahead, in gold position.

56

THE CRUELLEST WHISPER

Pearl's final event was beam. Ryan's was rings. For once, they were side by side, only ten metres between them across the mats. Pearl smiled at him. A gold medal awaited her. She was so far ahead of Jada-Rae in the scores now, she wouldn't even need to risk a Cazacu dismount. Ignoring the hulking presence of Coach Squibb on his shoulder, Ryan beamed back. More widely and freely than for a long time. Pearl wasn't the only gymnast from Bagley End Butterflies heading for a gold medal.

He stepped across the mats.

'You've got this,' he said, holding out his fist.

'And so do you,' replied Pearl, doing their exploding

fist bump.

Pearl watched after him as he went to chalk up. Her gaze wandered over to the rings. It was an impressively engineered piece of apparatus. A pair of wooden rings hung from straps suspended off a three-metre-high steel arch, secured by four wire cables screwed into the ground with metal tighteners. Ryan dipped into his final toe touch, then curled his fists in victory. Pearl curled her fists back. They could do it.

Then Pearl noticed her. Jada-Rae was kneeling by one of the tighteners, appearing to restrap the tape on her ankle. She stood up, walked to the next tightener and dropped down again. She adjusted the same piece of tape. She looked up and gave Pearl a slow smile.

'Pearl Bolton on beams,' called the announcer.

Pearl walked quickly back to the beam area, adrenaline pumping. What was Jada-Rae up to? Worries flooded her mind; she shook them away, trying to focus on her performance. She looked at the beam. Before her stood all her hopes and dreams. Out of the corner of her eye, she saw Jada-Rae approach. She draped an arm around Pearl's shoulder.

'Hey, I gave your buddy's ring tighteners a loosen. Thought it would make his last event more . . . dramatic. Amazing what you can do with the smallest of tools.' Pearl snorted. She didn't believe her. Then she thought uneasily of what Jada-Rae had done to Isla's bar. Pearl watched as Jada-Rae swaggered off and sat down beside Miss Cazacu.

'Final call, Pearl Bolton,' said the announcer irritably.

Pearl saluted. She wouldn't let Jada-Rae steal her victory like this. She focused on her mount, leaping up gazelle-like. She landed neatly. A bend of the legs. A twist to the left. She tiptoed along the length of the beam, like she was walking a tightrope. Jada-Rae was bluffing. Surely. This was exactly what she wanted. Pearl to be distracted. She stretched backwards until her fingers touched the suede, then tipped over, playing with her weight.

She glanced over at Ryan. Coach Squibb was approaching him, preparing to lift him on to the rings. It might be fine. Maybe they would still be strong enough with a loose tightener. Even if one wire cable burst loose, maybe the arch would hold firm. Unless he was mid-swing. She steadied herself for her backwards walkover, arching her neck back, willing herself to focus. But Ryan could be hospitalized, just like Isla. From upside down she sprung over. She landed perfectly, raising straight up into an arabesque. This was her moment. For a winning score, she needed to finish the routine without any big errors. She made a decision – the most winning decision she'd ever made.

Pearl leapt up, but not along the beam – she leapt away

and down. The judges stood up, confused. She sprinted towards the rings. Ryan was already in Coach Squibb's hands, reaching upwards, eyes on the rings. If he swung and something snapped it could bring dislocation, broken bones or worse. As she sprinted forward, she saw the confusion in his eyes.

'Stop! You'll fall.'

Coach Squibb froze, mid-heave.

'Get off there, you'll have everyone disqualified!' he glowered. 'We don't need more trouble.'

'What are you doing?' cried Miss Cazacu, rushing over.

'Check the apparatus.' Pearl pointed over at the tighteners. 'It's been tampered with.' The arena quietened in shock. Every head turned to watch. Ryan jumped down. They knelt down by the tighteners. Pearl shook them, inspected them left and right. They were firm. Totally safe. In fact, impossible to unscrew.

'They're fine, Pearl. It's safe.' Under his elasticated glasses, Ryan's eyes were full of concern.

'So it is,' she said, holding back tears. 'My mistake.' All the blood in her body seemed to drain away. She had been duped. There was no sabotage. No one would ever know what Jada-Rae had whispered in her ear.

Miss Cazacu shook her head in disbelief. Over on the team bench, Jada-Rae smiled and shrugged. The scoreboard changed, drawing their attention. Jada-Rae was in the lead, followed by three Russians. Up by Pearl's name, the word DISQUALIFIED flashed. There would be no podium for her now. She had failed in front of everyone she loved. She had broken her promise to Mum.

'You did that,' said Ryan. 'To keep me safe?'

'What's a medal between friends?' whispered Pearl, pulling a tight smile. 'Now win for both of us. Go, Bagley End Butterflies!'

She watched his performance, feeling like her foolish heart would break. Simple yet flawless, it was a masterclass in execution. Every hold was rock steady. Every handstand was totally vertical. Toes constantly pointed. A pencil-straight swallow position. Swings that you could set a stopwatch to. Pearl gasped as Ryan finished with a double tuck dismount. He landed, keeping his knees bent, his arms outstretched, until stillness settled. He straightened up safely. For the first time in his life, he was a true champion.

Tears sprung into Pearl's eyes, but they were tears of happiness. Though it hurt to lose, she realized something she should have known all along. Gymnastics was about more than scores. It was about seeing how high she could fly and how far she could leap, knowing there was someone there to catch her. The greatest win of all was to have her friend back.

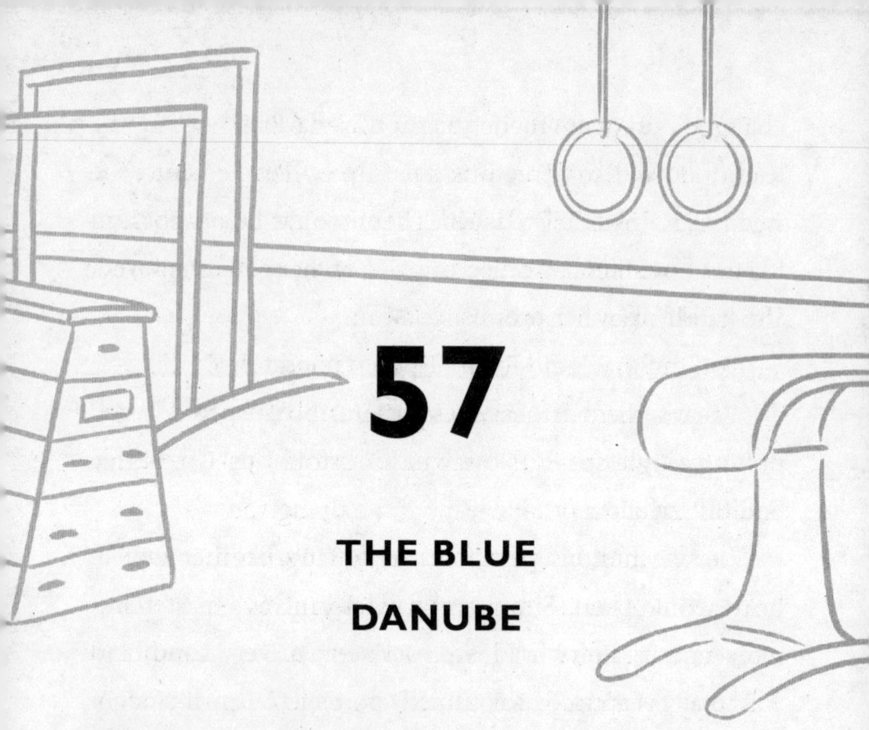

57

THE BLUE DANUBE

Pearl sat on the team benches, with a towel on her head. She refused all questions. She turned away from the camera crews. She didn't look beside her at where Ryan sat, squashed between Coach Squibb and Dr Pond. Because ahead of her Jada-Rae stood, at the edge of the floor square, ready to begin her floor routine. Back arched, she was the picture of success. She waved at the crowd, the row of international judges and finally the team benches, giving Pearl a cold-eyed smile. The green light flicked on. Up in the sound booth, Mrs Lulu raised a thumb. The arena speakers burst into life. Pearl crossed her arms. It was payback time.

The sound of energetic violins blared out. Strauss's 'The Blue Danube'. Jada-Rae took her first waltzing leap across the floor followed by a double backflip. The crowd roared.

Pearl slumped into a squat, drew her knees up and pressed them over her eyes in defeat.

'Don't worry . . . it's coming any second now,' mouthed Ryan across the benches, to Coach Squibb's confusion.

On cue, the speakers crackled to a stop. Jada-Rae didn't falter as she did a double leap with a flying split.

Over the audio came a voice. Jada-Rae's. Clear and cold. Pearl shot to her feet, beaming at Ryan. Never had she been more grateful for his passion for audio, his editing skills and his aptitude for computers. Especially Mrs Lulu's laptop, late at night, in a Parisian hotel suite.

'Look, this isn't just survival of the fittest. It's survival of the toughest. To win, you've got to be prepared to cut down the competition. By whatever means necessary. Be that injuries, psyching them out, unlucky falls or unfortunate stomach upsets.'

The arena had gone quiet. The uneven bars had ceased creaking. As the audio played, there were neither whoops, nor boings of springboards, nor thuds of landings. Not a soul clapped. Coach Squibb sheepishly took his hand off Ryan's shoulder. Miss Cazacu stood at the end, her face white. The judges looked shocked. In the sound booth, Mrs Lulu began arguing with the sound engineer. The line of sponsorship executives in the VIP box all stood up, phones out, ready to make calls. Jada-Rae kept going in her step-perfect routine. She turned at the corner of the floor square and tipped her chin up. Tears glistened on her cheeks. She sprinted forward, arms splayed out, and dived into a handstand. Despite knowing it was all over, she was a professional to the bitter end.

'Who do you think encouraged me to do this? Miss Cazacu doesn't care. None of them do. Not about you or any other gymnast I've taken out.'

The whole arena watched as Jada-Rae did a flying flip, twisting three hundred and sixty degrees. Twice. It was mastery. It was perfection. As they watched, they all listened. It was downfall. Jada-Rae finished her routine. She raised her arms in a victory that was total defeat.

58

THE LOCKET NECKLACE

Pearl went to sit beside Ryan. Neither Dr Pond nor Coach Squibb prevented her. Together they looked up at the big screen. The camera panned past the Russian gymnasts celebrating and zoomed in on the judging table. Every official in the building seemed to be clustered around it, like wasps around a puddle of Fruitogade. In the middle was Miss Cazacu. She stood up as Jada-Rae was brought before her. A microphone was pushed in front of her, but she didn't seem to notice. Her eyes were lasered on her star pupil.

'I demanded excellence. Not cheating. Why would you ever think I would do that, Jada-Rae? To my own gymnasts?'

Jada-Rae looked stunned.

'But . . . you said *win at all costs.*'

'I said you must sacrifice everything to win. Family time, fun, even love. Not your character though. I didn't expect that.'

Jada-Rae's bottom lip quivered.

'But I did it for you.'

'I did not teach you a thing, did I?' Miss Cazacu's voice was filled with sadness. 'I love seeing my gymnasts excel, not for the medals, but for how it changes them on the inside. I have seen it set unhappy souls free, give courage to the scared and turn nobodies into somebodies. And you, Jada-Rae. I saw it lift you up. With every error and correction, you learnt to believe in yourself. That's what made you a champion. So you would trust, deep inside, your body would perform what your heart commanded.'

'But the notes you sent me – on the gold-edged notepaper?' Jada-Rae's voice was panicked, confused. 'You encouraged me to sabotage the others. To expose their weaknesses. You congratulated me when I did.'

Now it was Miss Cazacu's turn to look confused.

'I sent you no notes.'

'You did, you did, every night under my pillow. Target this gymnast, eliminate that gymnast. You told me to.'

Jada-Rae was shaking now, like her skeleton was falling apart. 'You got Mrs Lulu to deliver them.' Something dawned on her. She spun round towards Mrs Lulu, who had come down to the team benches and picked up her bag, as if to leave.

Silence. 'Miss Cazacu didn't even know about it, did she?' A camera flash. Jada-Rae's eyes filled with tears. 'It was you who made Mo slip!'

'Lulu?' said Miss Cazacu, rotating around to face Mrs Lulu. Her voice was higher than ever. 'You tricked my star pupil into sabotaging my team? Why?'

A crooked smile creased Mrs Lulu's face. She slowly pulled out her locket necklace. She undid the clasp and held out the picture inside for all to see. The cameras zoomed in. On the big screen, a close-up showed a photo of a young gymnast with a shimmering leotard and an impeccable smile. The same girl in all the pictures of Mrs Lulu's photo gallery at Leaping Spires. Her daughter.

'I told you Allegra had talent. I put everything into her. Years of driving her to and from training. Sitting behind the viewing window, watching her repetitions. Thousands of pounds in leos, gym club memberships, coaching and goodness knows what else. I gave up a promising fashion career to help her succeed. I moved house. I put her gymnastics before my marriage. I became your assistant because I thought it would give her a better chance of success.'

'I don't understand,' said Miss Cazacu, her voice shaky.

'Trailing around after you, making your every whim happen. Yes, Miss Cazacu. No, Miss Cazacu. Cup of tea, Miss Cazacu? You might have created athletes, but I gave them style! Panache! Flair! Sophistication! When medals are won or lost over a tenth of a point, a beautiful leotard can give them the edge. Not that you ever appreciated what I brought.' Her eyes blazed with the bitterness of a woman wronged. 'I would have thought after everything I did for you, you would have done just one thing for me. Instead, you crushed my daughter's dream. You didn't select her for the team. She retired after that. Too old. My years of effort, wasted. She could have been a star, if it wasn't for you. So I decided your career should be destroyed just like Allegra's was.'

'I remember her, Allegra Sweet. Heavy on the artistry, light on the grit,' said Miss Cazacu, stepping around the table. She walked over to Mrs Lulu. She lowered her voice, but it was still loud enough for the microphones to catch it.

'Sometimes it's easier to believe you were wronged, that your daughter's medals were stolen from you, than face your greatest fear. That she was never champion material. No matter how many sequins and crystals you piled on to her, she was not gold in here.' Miss Cazacu touched her heart. 'You are dismissed from Leaping Spires. Effective immediately.'

The words hit like darts. Mrs Lulu raised her hand, as if to strike Miss Cazacu. Who did not flinch.

The cameras followed Mrs Lulu as she clutched her mouth and hurried to the exit.

Pearl looked over at Jada-Rae, who walked, sobbing, to the barriers. An unusually tall family dashed down the stands to her. The family that was in the photo in her bedside cabinet. Pearl remembered Jada-Rae's desperation to be the kid who was going somewhere, convinced that was the only way she'd be loved. And despite everything, Pearl felt more sorrow than hate for her.

Ryan pointed across to a shadowed corner where Miss Cazacu had retired. Out of the view of the cameras, a man in a Romanian tracksuit rushed over and took her in his arms. They kissed through his greying beard.

'I remembered why he looked familiar before. Zoltan Kiss. Olympic champion when Miss Cazacu was competing. They had to keep their love secret then, because they were in the same team, and now because they're rival coaches.'

'And I thought Miss Cazacu was a mole for the

Romanians,' said Pearl, shaking her head.

'Guess not everyone's guilty after all,' Ryan laughed. 'Statistically speaking.'

'Maybe not everyone's innocent either,' said Pearl, laughing back.

59

THE RAISED FLAG

Ryan stood on the podium. For once, he didn't look awkward. He looked like this was his plan all along. Behind him the Union Jack was raised. He bent down to receive his gold medal, allowing himself a small smile. Beside him in bronze position, Hamish put an arm over Ryan's shoulder, too happy to hold grudges. From the stands, Dad waved his banner. Max blew a vuvuzela. Gloria clapped and beat her fist in the air. There was a delight in her cheering, like she'd just realized her boy was going to be OK in this world.

'I always thought he didn't believe in himself, when really it was me who was frightened for him,' said Gloria, not taking her eyes off him as she clapped. She blinked away tears.

Beside her, Pearl bounced up and down. She couldn't have been more proud. Maybe Ryan had known the right way to win all along. By pushing himself, but never too far. By training safe, training smart and trusting the medals would come. By putting friendship first.

Ryan steadily made his way over. Pearl whooped, realizing she might finally agree with him. Gymnastics gave her the power to snuff out gravity, fly like a bird and draw rainbows in the air. There was no medal she'd swap for that.

He straddled over the arena barriers, ignoring the photographers and reporters. His feet were pointed a little less inwards as he walked up the stands to Gloria. He stood before her like he'd grown a good centimetre.

'I, Ryan, am a winner. I, Ryan, always was. I, Ryan, promise never to do a stupid affirmation ever again.' Gloria almost knocked him over as she pulled him in for a hug. The photographers and reporters caught up. Cameras flashed.

'I, Gloria,' she shouted over the reporters' questions, 'promise we can take the rest of the summer off. No gymnastics, just like you asked.' Ryan laughed, and calmly began an interview. He spoke into the microphone like he'd done this all his life, gently plugging his podcast.

'But . . .' said Pearl, panicking at the thought of August without Ryan at gymnastics. Gloria rubbed Pearl's back.

'You know what your mum once told me? A holiday is worth ten thousand backflips. Maybe you should try it too.'

Pearl thought for a moment. Suddenly she felt a pang of missing, for summers gone and cartwheels on the beach with Mum. She looked at Dad.

'How about that trip to the seaside?' she suggested.

'I'll make dumplings for tea every day,' Dad belly-laughed.

'Yes!' yelped Max. 'We can get a beach hut.'

'I'll teach you cartwheels,' decided Pearl.

'Are we invited?' Ryan asked Gloria.

''Course you are,' said Dad. 'You're pretty much family.' He and Gloria looked at each other so tenderly that Pearl and Ryan giggled. Perhaps their parents were becoming more than just friends.

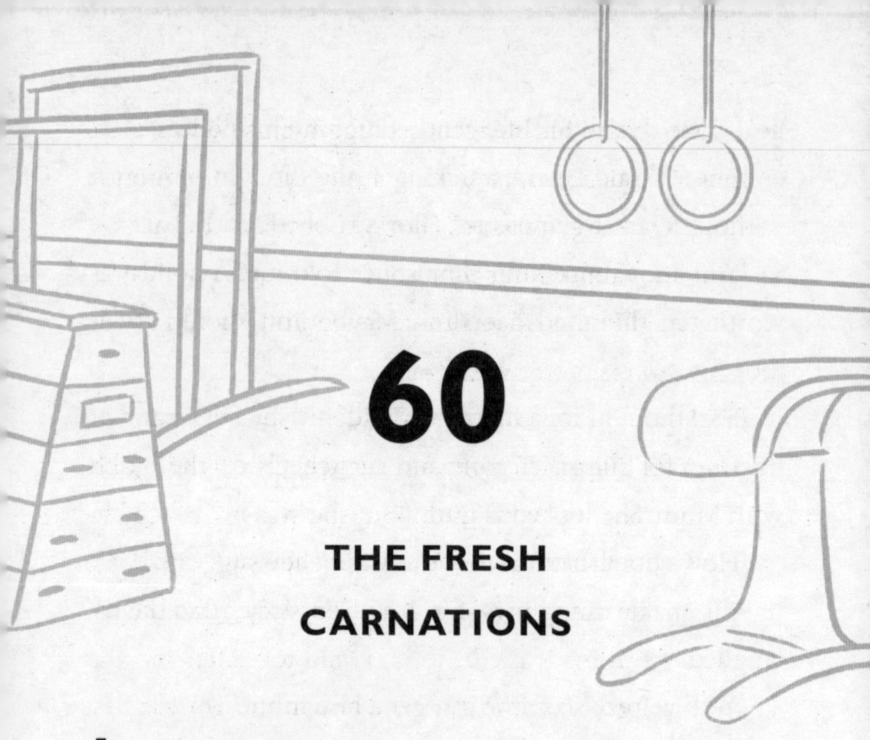

60

THE FRESH CARNATIONS

It was raining when Pearl returned to Bagley End Cemetery. It dripped off stone and ran in little rivulets along the gravel paths. Pearl picked her way through the old graves. To the new ones in shiny granite. To the grave that never left her thoughts.

Renshu Chui-Bolton
Wife to one,
Mother to two,
Inspiration to gymnasts,
Ray of sunshine to all.

The sequins had either faded in the sun or slid off. They

lay scattered around. Leaning on the granite was a fresh bunch of carnations. A few steps back, arms curled round knees on the wet grass, sat Ryan. He stood up quickly, shaking the rain off his spiky hair.

'Oh,' said Pearl, suddenly understanding who had been leaving flowers every week.

'Hi.'

The rain filled their awkward silence, then Ryan spoke.

'I know she was your mum. But she was my coach,' he said. 'I miss her too. She always believed I could do anything. She never had any doubt I'd stick a landing or nail a move. It made me believe I could too. After she was gone it just got so hard to believe any more.' For the first time, Pearl connected Mum's death to when Ryan's worries about safety began.

From the inside pocket of his tracksuit he pulled out his medal. He stood up, unwinding the ribbon.

'This one's for you, Coach Renshu.' He stepped forward and hung it on the gravestone.

'She would have been so proud of you,' said Pearl, eyes on the dangling metal.

'You too. You gave up gold for your friend. That'd make you a winner in her book.'

He gave her one of those looks. Pearl felt like her heart might shred.

'Sun's definitely not shining today,' he said, looking up at the rain clouds.

'And that's OK,' said Pearl. Though they never ever hugged, today they did. It felt golden.

Ryan walked away, passing a burly man approaching. A man who rarely visited the cemetery. Dad walked slowly to the grave and laid down a bunch of sunflowers.

'I'm sorry I haven't visited your mum much,' he said, staring straight ahead. 'Or come to your practices. It's been hard.' He wrapped his arms around Pearl. He smelt of frying pan grease, laundry and love. The hug seemed to extend until Pearl felt a prickling in her eyes.

'I let Mum down,' she said in the quietest of voices. 'I promised that I'd shine brightly for her. I had to win gold but I didn't.'

Dad held her at arm's length.

'Pearl Bolton. You *always* shined for her.' He stroked her hair. 'Not by winning medals. That's not what she meant,' he said, tears welling in his eyes. 'It wasn't something you had to become. You shine every day. As a daughter, a big sister and a best friend, as well as just for being you. The cartwheels weren't what made her love you.' Pearl gave Dad the tightest squeeze before he left, feeling a lightness she hadn't felt in a year.

Once the cemetery was empty, Pearl sat cross-legged in

front of the grave. She had brought neither sequins nor superglue today. And she did no handstands, nor flick-flacks.

Instead, she closed her eyes. She didn't say anything to Mum. And Mum, as always, said nothing back. Pearl listened to the plip-plop of rain under the grey sky. She felt it on her skin, slipping down her neck under her tracksuit. Slowly, the rain mixed with her tears. All was quiet save the traffic from the Caernarfon Road and the sound of her grief.

When she had finished, she stood up and wiped her eyes. She would go home and pack for their trip. While her suitcase was out, she'd put away something special. Her lucky leotard would be safely stored in the attic. A memory she'd always cherish. Then tomorrow, she would light up the world with her shine, but this time in a different way. They'd pack the car and drive to the beach, laughing at Dad singing out of tune. Gloria would put up a windbreak and lay out cheese sandwiches, fruit cake and gallons of Fruitogade. Ryan would record the waves for a podcast on rest and relaxation for gymnasts. Dad would cook dumplings on a burner in the beach hut. Pearl would teach Max the joy of cartwheels – limbs outstretched, free-wheeling with gravity on the sand until they collapsed in a dizzy, giggling heap.

She bent over, kissed her fingers, then gently pressed them on the gravestone.

And it felt OK to say goodbye.

CREDITS

Editing by Shalu Vallepur and Rachel Leyshon

Cover direction by Rachel Hickman

Illustration by Natalie Smillie

Cover design by Steve Wells

Copy-editing by Jenny Glencross

Publishing management by Esther Waller

Rights direction by Elinor Bagenal

Publicity by Laura Smythe and Ruth Hoey

Agenting by Jodie Hodges

Gymnastic advice by Libby May and the ChalkBucket community

Cartwheel instruction by Southwark Gymnastics

Draft reading by Zak, Lizzie, Solveig and Mary Emerson, Anna Sweet, Dan Gifford, Suzy Ross

Candid feedback by Arthur and Caspar

Support in stories and everything else by Zak

ALSO BY ELOISE SMITH

SISTER TO A STAR

LIGHTS. CAMERA. KIDNAP!

Evie is forever crossing swords with her twin. While she practises her after-school fencing, Tallulah is winning movie auditions.

Neither could have guessed their worlds would collide.

When Tallulah goes to Hollywood, Evie goes too – as her sister's identical . . . stand-in. But that changes when the film needs some all-action swordplay.

Soon Evie's the one enjoying the limelight. That is, until Tallulah goes missing . . .

A fabulous middle-grade adventure all about the highs and lows of sibling relationships, the exciting sport of fencing, and the fabulous world of film-making.

THE SCHOOL LIBRARIAN